SKELMERSDALE

LOVERS FOR A DAY

Also by Ivan Klíma

LOVERS FOR A DAY

Ivan Klíma

Translated from the Czech by
Gerald Turner

Granta Books
London

Granta Publications, 2/3 Hanover Yard, London N1 8BE

First published in Great Britain by Granta Books 1999

The stories in *Lovers for a Day* have been translated from the following collections: *Milenci na jednu noc* (Lovers for One Night), *Milenci na jeden den* (Lovers for One Day), *Milostne rozhovory* (Intimate Conversations)

A CIP catalogue record for this book
is available from the British Library.

1 3 5 7 9 10 8 6 4 2

Typeset by M Rules
Printed and bound in Great Britain by
Mackays of Chatham plc

CONTENTS

Lovers for One Night

EXECUTION OF A HORSE

1

A bright violet flash. She half opened her eyes at the light. A storm, she realized, an early morning storm. The windows rattled slightly. She was gripped by anxiety. I ought to run to Mummy for shelter, it automatically occurred to her, but I can't do that any more. It's been ages since I could! She shut her eyes tightly, and strangely that feeling from the time when she could still run for shelter came back to her, that feeling of reassurance. Maybe it was because of the storm, or because she was close to dreaming, or because it hadn't really been so long since she used to run to her mother.

The feeling was so strong that she actually reached out into the empty space beside her and thought she was touching a hand and hearing quiet breathing. Having started with a storm, what sort of day would it turn out to be?

When she awakes for the second time, it feels like full morning

3

already. She can feel the warmth on her eyelids and the sound of an argument comes through the wall.

She pads across the parquet in her bare feet: her toes sense the morning and how the day stands – it's my free day – and once more there is the twinge of realization that she no longer knows what to blame him on or where to go to avoid him. But why should I avoid him? I simply won't think about him. After all, it was what I wanted too. We weren't a good match anyway – even if he hadn't done what he did.

Even so she can't stop feeling sorry for herself. How could he have done it? How could he have deceived her when she loved him and he said he loved her too? I could never have done it.

Love, she reflects, true love, is unbreakable. It is complete and everlasting, even though I may never ever know it: not everyone is destined to experience true love. And she feels a sudden pang of regret. Just outside the window drops of water glisten on the dry branch which reminds her of an owl. You think I'll never know it, that nothing like that happens these days, but I'll bide my time, and then one morning like this one he'll lean over me, my beloved, and put his hand here, right here, and he'll be here at my side, all of him, and his warmth will enfold me.

And she feels lonely, very lonely. There is nothing else she need think about and she is utterly dejected. When she has dressed she quietly climbs the narrow winding staircase that emerges in front of a low door underneath the rafters. Here there is a room she can escape to. It's not even a proper room. It used to be just a mansard: it has a sloping roof and a small, high window, starting at neck level and ending at the height of her forehead. The room contains nothing but childhood junk,

a tin washbasin to bring water from the passage, and a cupboard, an ironing board with a hole burnt in the cover, a
rocking chair and a great big ball of blue twine – not of hemp,
let alone paper, but of some synthetic material: twine for tying
up parcels and battered suitcases, as well as for hanging washing, and those in despair. It now hangs on a nail and its free
end swings to and fro almost imperceptibly, rather scarily in
this room with the door and window closed. But it calms her
to sit in the rocking chair watching the world see-saw up and
down.

It's still the early morning and the sun shines in her eyes;
above it the heavens with two clouds that sail slowly past. A
shoreless lake with boats sinking, a blue desert with a caravan of
white elephants. I can sail and wander. In the complete silence
she can hear the sand noiselessly piling up into blue dunes, and
slowly, like a mirage, the outline of the first tower emerges, and
a chimney thrusting skywards and an enormous plinth for an
enormous statue, with no statue, that marvellous landmark;
and lower and lower, below the roofs – this is my city – down
to the river, and above the river coloured prisms with cello-
phane and trams (chipped thermos flasks), motor cars and
converging dots just moving – those are people – if I were to go
down there I'd be like them and maybe someone would be glad
and say, Stay here now, don't go back. No thank you, I'm
happy here. This is where I'm happiest of all. Here I'm all
alone when I feel like it and I won't be if I don't feel like it.
And up again: the owl-shaped branch again, and higher and
higher up to the outline of the last tower and the chimney
thrusting skywards. It's still early morning and the sun is rising.
The day had such a pallid start – but now, now it's like a tree
growing out of the damp earth, like a field, like a roof facing

5

away from the city. She would like to do something: I have to do something on a day like this. I'll put on that white pleated skirt and then I could go for a swim – with Markéta probably – or just go off somewhere, go and thumb a lift from the last tram stop, all on my own – why not, someone's bound to stop and give me a lift somewhere. And maybe he'll be young and afterwards he'll say, Actually I'm not going anywhere, it was just a whim this morning. And I'll reply, It wasn't just your whim, it was mine as well. Except that it'll turn out to be some dreary married man instead. But that doesn't matter, I'll get dropped off somewhere where there are some rocks and climb up them. And then when I get to the top, it'll be like it used to be with us, only I'll lie down in the warm clovery grass all by myself, far from any path, and wait.

And she quietly slips out of the room that is more like a mansard and in which only the end of the ball of twine will now swing to and fro almost imperceptibly behind the closed window and the closed door.

2

Heading for the tram in her white pleated skirt and green blouse she has to pass the old dump with BEWARE FALLING MASONRY and two hideous angels over the door. She hesitates briefly and then walks in past the one-armed watchman. I oughtn't to really, I'll end up bumping into that old so-and-so of hers I'm not supposed to know about, though these days she doesn't make too much of an effort to conceal it. Poor Mum with that bald fat old slob. She knocks on the door and then opens it. From within emerges the confused din of typewriters with the pale blue glow of the strip-lighting and the stench of cigarettes and cheap coffee. But she stays outside.

'What did you want, Kateřina?'

'Nothing in particular.'

Sallow cheeks, pouches under her eyes, lipstick meticulously applied – everything about her is meticulous, in fact. Her hair recently dyed black. She's still trying to be attractive.

'I'm going out for the day, Mum.'

'Who with?'

'On my own, Mum!'

'Fibber!'

'No, really on my own. Don't worry.'

She looks round and steps away from the door slightly. 'You're telling me fibs again. Why do *you* have to as well?'

'I'm not fibbing. We've broken up.'

'Well take good care of yourself.'

'Why don't you believe me?'

'Don't cause me grief, Kateřina.'

The door opens. The witch with the coffee pot lets out some of the pale blue light and typewriter din. Is that you, Kateřina – how are you – fine thanks – it suits you, every inch the young lady, where did you buy the skirt, and you're bigger than your Mum, come on show me, you really are – it's my hair that does it, I tease it.

'You're not up to something are you, Kateřina?'

'No, I'm not, really Mum.'

She has powdered the wrinkles round her eyes – for that slob, but what's she supposed to do, now that Daddy avoids her? 'No, really, Mum. It's lovely out.'

'What's up, Kateřina? You're being distant, somehow. Don't stay out late.'

LOVERS FOR A DAY

'No, I won't.'

She says goodbye to the one-armed watchman. Outside it is bright and sunny and oddly deserted. The rush hour is over. He's probably just getting up. They get up late in student residences. If only I'd been able to study too. I'd have enjoyed it: preferably biology or literature. But those two would have had to keep me for the four years and where would they have found the money, those penniless pen-pushers? He has to pay for his tart and she has to keep her slob, if she's going to have any fun any more – I'd sooner hang myself. No thermos flask anywhere, I'll make a phone call while I'm waiting.

The phone box is empty. She makes herself comfortable, an elbow resting on the shelf and a foot on the ledge in the wall. I've got quite nice legs, really, the girls envy me them when I undress, but I've got only one twenty-five heller piece. I could try calling you but what's the point – it's just a game; to have you come to the phone and shout, Who's that – Katka? Or is it you, Libuše? How could you have done it to me. You could have let me know, at least. Not that it would make any difference. What if I called Markéta? Have you heard the news? Ota and I have broken up. Would you believe it, he's been carrying on with that PE instructor of theirs for the past two years and I didn't know a thing. That time during the holidays when he said he was canoeing – that was with her. I told him myself: there's no point. I could never do anything like that – we didn't hit it off anyway. You were always amazed that he and I could, that I never seemed myself with him. It's only now that I realize it. I feel great now, believe me, although before . . .

There's a man knocking on the door of the booth. Every inch the gentleman. I bet he hits his children. Wait a bit, I'll let you have my twenty-five heller piece, I didn't use it. Sorry.

The thermos flask is half empty. I'll stay out on the platform; it's getting hot. She goes and stands behind the driver and ponders on love for a while. Living without love is not the worst thing: the worst thing is where love has fallen to pieces and is no longer love but a burden. She is pleased with herself for having managed to escape a love that was sure to turn into a burden.

She gets off one stop early and walks past the ugly student residence – his window is closed and the bottom half is stuck over with paper. But she doesn't stop even for a second. She feels fancy-free, liberated: the whole day is spread out in front of her, her whole life is spread out in front of her – days unimaginable, full of promise. But she is not even thinking about that now, just about today, which is also full of promise.

A car soon pulled up for her, a private car, no less. The suede-jacketed driver opened the door and looked her over quickly. Obviously satisfied, he asked, 'Where are you off to?'

'I don't mind.'

'If you don't mind, you don't mind.'

He drove fast and talked non-stop. He was an expert on animal skins, apparently, and bought and sold them all over the world. He was a bit too tall and bony for her taste, and probably too old as well, even though he was under forty. He spoke very slowly and deliberately, which appealed to her. That was the way she imagined people spoke who had seen things and were possibly important in some way too. It had not been very sensible to have spent all her time with Ota recently, as if he were the only person in the world. Love is definitely the greatest happiness, but at the same time it swallows you up and at the very moment you feel you are living to the full you actually stop living. Countless possible loves, moments and opportunities pass you by and they might be more important and more fulfilling than what you have at that moment, but you're unaware of them.

In the fields the corn was not yet ripe. The man had now fallen silent. The names of unfamiliar villages, the air shimmering above the road's surface, a narrow valley and wooded hilltops. If only I could just keep on going like this: the whole day and again the next day and never return, never return anywhere.

The man asked, 'And you really don't care where you're going?'

'Really!' she exclaimed.

'I'll show you something.'

Then, even though he really ought to have waited for her reaction, he turned sharply off the main road and sped on in a cloud of whitish dust.

She hadn't the slightest idea where he intended to take her and not to know where you were heading or what might happen was quite exciting. The car took another turn and they were now travelling along a rough field track in the direction of three solitary buildings.

The man got out, opened the door and quite unnecessarily offered her his hand, giving hers a squeeze in the process. Only now was his full height apparent – he was a born basketball player: 'I bet this is something you've never seen before.'

They entered a bare and deserted yard containing only a rusting pump and several rolls of barbed wire in one corner. She found the emptiness rather oppressive. It was a farm made for a murder. The man went ahead of her with long – rather ludicrously long – and important strides. They passed under a low gateway and suddenly found themselves in a strange, incredible township of thousands of wooden cages. 'Wait here a moment!' The stench of animal excrement hung in the air, as well as another smell she could not place.

In front of a building that resembled a garage with an excessively high opening – more like a hangar for a single forgotten aeroplane – stood a grey horse tied to a post with the bark still on it.

She had never before seen a colour like it – like black soil covered in a layer of hoar frost. She wanted to go over to that beautiful creature, but her companion was already returning, taking those ludicrously long and important strides. Actually, she was pleased he was on his way back, because a strange, inexplicable melancholy had settled on the place. Hurrying behind him came a bald fat man with a bunch of keys.

'What marvellous guests . . .' said the fat man. 'So the young lady is curious about our mink,' and they passed through the barbed wire entrance between the cages standing on high crossed legs, in which solitary brown creatures ran here and there in confusion.

Her companion was openly delighted at the sight of them and talked about 'those carnivores' ceaselessly – maybe for her benefit, but no doubt also to show off to the other man. And so they wended their way through the maze of solitary cells from which the inmates had no escape, destined to live for just nine months, until they were at their most magnificent, and she felt pity well up within her as it did whenever she saw a captive animal.

They reached a row of cages, each containing a pair of the creatures darting to and fro. This is where we keep the sick ones, her companion explained. They recover quicker in company than on their own. And the two men continued their rounds. Perhaps they had forgotten about her and so she stayed by the couples that illness had redeemed from solitary confinement. It is often only solitude that drives people into love, and in fact people waver between freedom and solitude – except that most of the time they lose their freedom without escaping solitude. I must have read that somewhere, but now I know it, now I actually feel it.

The two men were now lost in the maze and she retraced her steps to the previous row of stinking animal cages and was suddenly seized by a very powerful feeling – an intuition almost – that this wasn't going to be any ordinary day: it was a day when even love might come her way. She was so convinced of it that if the lanky man in the suede jacket whose name she didn't even know were to approach her at that moment and say, I love you, she would most likely fall in love with him, totally and absolutely – until she came out at the spot where they had entered and she caught sight of the grey horse in front of her.

It stood there, head hanging. And as she approached it – she had never been afraid of large animals, only of spiders, caterpillars and frogs – she noticed that one of its eyes was covered in an opaque film and it struck her that it must be an old horse and that the layer of hoar frost was in fact no more than a sign of age. It was attached by the shortest of ropes, really a long rope but mostly tied round the stake, and its forelegs were bound together with thick twine. It too was a prisoner, but she felt greater pity for it than for the paltry creatures in the cages. There was something human about its remaining eye – though it couldn't be wisdom. Maybe it was sorrow or anxiety; maybe just pain or exhaustion. Exhaustion most likely.

Rummaging in her handbag she found some sweets and the horse nuzzled them wearily from her palm with its grey lips while gazing at her motionlessly with its one eye. She placed her hand on its mane and stayed at its side, feeling now the pulse of the large creature and hearing its breath, while its scent enveloped her. She suddenly felt something akin to tenderness or even love, or at least warm, comforting friendship. 'You lovely beast,' she murmured, 'my little brother, you silly old horse,' and the horse's breathing seemed to slow down and a tremor ran through its enormous body.

Then the doors of the strange hangar opened in front of her and out stepped two men in blue-and-white striped overalls.

'He's been getting friendly, the old so-and-so,' said one of them.

She had to step back several paces and she observed how the men unwound the rope from the raw timber post and dragged the horse towards the open doorway.

She wanted to shout something after them but at that moment the horse stopped, braced itself and began to neigh.

'Come on, you stubborn old bastard,' they yelled and the horse stood, nailed to the spot, tossing its old silvery head and neighing. One of the fellows turned towards her and said in a friendly voice, 'The beast has caught the scent of blood. That's put it off!'

And then suddenly she realized what the two men were and that she ought to do something to save the horse, though she knew she could do nothing.

All she could do was leave and that's what she ought to do. At least she wouldn't witness what was going to happen. But she couldn't budge from the raw timber post and she stared numbly as the men lowered a pulley from the roof of the hangar, threw a rope over the pulley wheel, made a noose with the other end and put it round the horse's neck. And she watched rigidly as the men started to pull with all their might, while the horse also strained its every muscle, all its veins standing out. And then she saw the horse gradually rear on its hind legs – in ghastly human fashion, pulled by the terrible rope, she saw its hooves first pound the earth in terror and then just thrash the air, heard the roar of the creature, the despairing roar of a horse, its cry of anguish, its vain entreaties, a roar not of foreboding but of certainty. And she watched the horse as with strange, unnatural leaps it drew nearer to the hangar's gaping maw. Have pity! Oh, God! At least let them close the doors. And indeed at that very moment the doors closed behind the two men and the condemned beast and she waited, although she didn't know what for, and then it came: not a cry, not a roar, but a thud, the dull, resounding thud of a heavy body falling on to a stone floor. So that was the end. Suddenly she could no longer feel her own body. She drifted in the air, before sinking on to the soft, sandy soil. But she still held on limply to the wooden post, her hands above her head, and pressed her lips to the rough, hard bark. She dug her teeth into the bark until she tasted the bitterness of the wood beneath.

And the thud swelled and spread out, resounding within her until it drowned out everything that was and everything that would be; she was sure the sound would never cease, because it was not the sort of sound made by things but a sound that came out of the void, from between slightly closed doors: it was the voice of the darkness into which all defenceless creatures are dragged.

Then she heard the creak of the hangar doors again and looked up in a sort of vain and macabre hope, but all she saw were the two men in the blue-and-white overalls, each pulling a small cart on which lay a metal washtub covered by a bloody canvas. So she stood up and even though she still could not feel her own body she set off with strange, unnatural leaps into the void in front of her.

3

Towards evening it started to cloud over again and the sun disappeared behind a smoky screen. The soldiers dropped her off as soon as they reached the city limits and shouted something at her in parting. That morning she had never suspected she would be back so early, while it was still fully light, or in such a frame of mind. Where shall I go now? I must go and find someone. I could go to a film – but go to the cinema on my own? Anyway I have to eat something. I'll have something to eat and then I'll call Markéta, but what will I talk to her about? A squalid eating place in a side street. Sit at a table on my own? But I'm hardly going to go home and sit looking at the pair of them.

She sits at a bare table. The grubby waiter arrives carrying mugs of beer, and a bowl of tripe soup for her. Her fingers tremble slightly. I'm really hungry. At least I'm eating and I'm able to eat, even if it's vile, disgusting meat.

She wants to think about something, about some book or film at least, instead of about the man in the suede jacket, the township of little wooden cages, the stench . . . And here it is standing in front of her with its grey coat and lank mane. It's no longer tied up but grazing freely, tossing its one-eyed head, and the meadow stretches from horizon to horizon and the horizon is dark, like a line run through the night. A corpse-faced man stares at her from the next table.

'Are you a student?'

'No.'

'Come and sit over here, then.'

'I've got a bowl of soup here.' And she doesn't feel like sitting next to the man, even though it makes no difference in the end. He looks a bit like Mum's old slob. I expect that's the way they lounge about. Poor Mum, when he touches her afterwards with those yellow talons of his.

'It looks as though you're a student after all.' His voice is high-pitched, almost effeminate. 'You don't want to sit with a man.' But I expect Mum is miserable about being left on her own. She needs more than just me. She misses love. So that's what that love is, the divine love they croon about. She took her soup and moved to the man's table.

'Are you a sales girl?'

'No!'

'I thought so. You're a student.'

'And what business is it of yours?' she snaps. If she were a student . . . but what difference does it make. What difference does it make what I am, what we happen to be at this moment – and she hears the echoing thud; it comes out of nowhere and no one seems to hear it – when we know what we will be one day.

'I could have gone to college too. Only they didn't send me there. I had to become a carter. And I can't stand those smart alecs,' he trilled. 'They're always showing off. What would they be without us? You're a secretary, then?'

'I'm nothing,' she says and it was true: nothing sipping tripe soup. But what will I be? Or will I stay being nothing until the moment when . . . no, I won't think about it.

'But we had some fun with them last year on Petřín Hill. We lit them up with rockets and pulled them out of the bushes.'

'What were they doing?'

'What were they doing? What were they doing . . .' and suddenly she remembers the little room almost up in the sky with the rocking chair and the window that starts at neck level and ends at the height of your forehead, and the enormous ball of blue twine whose free end is always swaying to and fro. She tries to remember when she was last up there and finds it impossible to believe that moment in the distant past had been that very morning.

'They'd already elected a prime minister,' the man piped up. 'They had it all worked out, the whole government and the central committee.'

'Did you beat them up?'

'Hold on, hold on,' he rebuked her. 'I'm asking the questions here.' Then he said, 'If my son went to college, he wouldn't bugger about like that lot. You ought to see what they get up to in those student halls. They take some tart or other . . .'

She had finished her soup at last. I must leave, get up and go somewhere, but where? I'll go home, but where . . . Or I'll go to his place. He fancies me a bit, or he used to. Except we've split up. I can't go and see him . . .

'You're a hairdresser, that's what you are! If you fancy making a bit on the side,' the man suddenly said in his high effeminate voice; his eyes were almost popping out of his head and he spoke rapidly. 'I don't live far from here and it wouldn't be anything – you'd only have to take off your skirt . . . Just watch,' he burst out, 'just you watch, Miss!' He went over to the cracked counter and put a five-crown coin down on the sheet of glass covering the wafers and chocolate biscuits.

'Don't worry about him,' the barman said to her. 'He's a bit of a, you know, cripple. He can't whatsname, you see,' and he dashed here and there between the tables.

Afterwards, as she climbs the steps to the student residence and passes the scarred corner of the building and the badly-painted railing, that familiar sense of hope starts to come back. He might still love her, even if she doesn't know what it means any more, love. But maybe he is expecting me and when I arrive he'll say, What have you been doing the whole week? I'm glad you're here. I'm not even sure why I'm here. It's just that I was lying there with my head in the sand and it just occurred to me that you will be kind to me, for a little while at least, even though you don't love me, and that you'll pay attention to me even when I don't say anything. In the passage there are two lit gas burners and a black student in white plimsolls and purple boxer shorts, and from behind a closed door the sound of a jazz trumpet.

'So you've come, then? You've seen sense, after all!' The cocksure star of the parallel bars in a tracksuit that had shrunk slightly in the shoulders. 'It was daft to sulk like that. You know how things are nowadays. You mustn't take it that way . . .'

The bottom half of the windows pasted over with photos, a jumble of discarded textbooks and study materials, sporting trophies all over the walls, a carved ox horn, and on a shelf a glass box painted with flowers and birds that's used as an ashtray.

'You're such a little girl still, Katka. You're always thinking about things you shouldn't, even when they're nothing to do with you.'

'But it is do with me when you're going out with someone else.'

'Don't be daft. All that matters is what there is between the two of us. Nothing else.'

And silence. The jazz trumpet from the passage. On the other side of the door the black student whistles a monotonous melody, outside the window it is evening. They chased them all over Petřín Hill, but I'm not a student, I won't build bridges, I won't reel off the names of kings or dynasties or study nine symphonies and it makes no difference, no difference at all. My kingdoms are white and pink cards in a hall with pale blue light and brushing off my skirt every single day at four-thirty. I'll brush off my skirt tomorrow and live in hope of a glimmer of merciful consideration if he happens to turn up. I'll wait outside the gate looking here and there and just go on waiting patiently, assenting now and then to clumsy minor indignities and to major deceptions like your current one, and go on waiting and waiting and waiting until the day when the two men in blue-and-white stripes arrive and toss a rope over and start to pull . . . No, I don't want to think about it, about what is going to come, what has to come, I just don't want to think about it.

'This is the third day here on my own already,' he said. 'After we've waited so long for it you had to go and sulk. Have you had something to eat?'

He's got some wine in the cupboard – the cheapest kind, naturally – and yesterday he came second in the rings in the assessment competition.

'It's time I was going.'

However she sits on the very dirty bed, the other bed is made and as level as a coffin. I'll go over and sit on it and just watch you. I don't feel like staying here, but where am I to go?

And so she drinks some wine, cheap and sharp, that she doesn't like at all and doesn't even bring much relief, just a slight drowsiness and a gradual blurring of the day and the days. Now you can talk about what you like now you can touch me and kiss me.

'Why did you do it? Why did you run away?'

'You know why.'

'You're like a little kid, Katka. What is it you're after?'

He goes and switches off the light. We're trapped in the dark like the mink, outside the window the lights from other windows. Now I see why they pasted over the bottom of the windowpanes. And a jazz trumpet from the other side of the wall.

'I'll switch on the radio so they won't hear . . .'

'Won't hear what?'

'You *are* daft, Katka. Or do you just put it on?'

He carries her easily and now they lie side by side, the radio is playing, someone is walking along the passage; it's bound to be the black guy in the purple boxer shorts. The jazz trumpet has fallen silent. If only it were quiet I would hear your breathing. God, I'm here next to you, what am I doing here? But I had to go somewhere, I didn't want to stay on my own. That's why I'm here, for one night at least. What choice did I have for tonight? And you'll indulge me for a little while, for this evening and this night. We've been lovers for one night. Say something at least. Don't stay silent – I feel uneasy with this strange music in a strange bed. And they lie here side by side. He kisses her, You're really pretty, little girl, come closer to me. – I'd like to see your face. – Come closer to me, okay? – Say you love me. – You're daft to ask me like that.– I'm daft to have come. – No, just daft to ask me like that.

20

But I do really love you and I'd tell you if you were to say it, but you don't say anything, just let your hands wander all over my body and nothing, nothing – why don't you take off your skirt? – but I'm glad, you lift me out of this day, you lift me up to you, maybe that feeling of happiness will come after all, so kiss me: I want to so much, I want to, my darling.

And so now they lie side by side half naked. It is stifling with such a low ceiling and the windows closed. He explores her body, pleased that she came by. The music has given way to a voice that intones gloomily . . . *qui est aux cieux! Que ton nom soit sanctifié* . . . her eyes are half closed and she is waiting for that moment, intent on it, and her eyes staring inwards watch every movement of her heart and pulse and suddenly from out of the depths of the night there comes the sound of a hollow thud and the deafening roar of doors opening, and the two of them are already waiting, arms open, smiling; the ropes rise upwards, the nooses swaying delightfully; how beautiful you are, your body's like silk, what for, for loving, what for, and the two of them are already swaggering over to her, show me your head, your throat is all white even in the dark, what for, for loving, silence, the priest has finished his prayers – silence and the sound of an organ.

'You're crying, Katka. What for?'

They are gone. Outside the window lighted windows. You lie at my side wearily the way all lovers lie, that's the way it is, and they leave and are lost, and they will return, the two stripy guys, and they'll hang around and one day they'll get to me too and the rope will start to chafe against my throat, and I'm rising upwards, for ever and for good, and you do nothing to hold me back, nobody holds me back, no one and nothing, and so the doors will close for ever, I know now, now I've realized it. Everything is clear to me.

'You're daft, Kateřina, you'll like it next time.'

4

There is total darkness and silence. The two of them are at home asleep – if Mum were to wake up, I expect we'd both have a cry, but what's the point, she's got her own . . . The same old homecoming, how many homecomings like this. So she doesn't even open the door but climbs the narrow winding staircase. The roof slopes down and the window is small and high and there is nothing here but childhood junk and a tin washbasin to bring water from the passage, and a cupboard, an ironing board with a hole burnt in the cover, a rocking chair and a great big ball of blue twine, not of hemp, let alone paper, but of some synthetic material that is much stronger than the strongest natural material, twine for tying up parcels of old rags and battered suitcases, as well as for hanging washing and those in despair.

She is tired. It is a strange, hopeless exhaustion that does not even desire sleep. Besieged by this exhaustion she switches on the light. It's odd to think that she was in this room yesterday morning. It's as if it all happened long ago, and she was standing at the end of it, or rather as if she was already standing at the beginning of a completely new time. She undresses slowly although she has yet to pull out the bed. On her skirt she discovers the shameful dark red stain, now almost black. It was such a beautiful skirt. And she feels like weeping over the white pleated skirt, over her tiredness and over herself, and she goes out into the passage and fills the washbasin with water. Then she takes the big ball of blue twine, but she has scarcely unwound a few metres when she is overcome with revulsion and rewinds it. And when she has washed off the stain she hangs the skirt over the ironing board. What am I to do now?

She switches off the light and sits down in the rocking chair, and at that moment it strikes her that love is actually like life. You know it's going to end badly, that it's going to end too soon and there is no hope of its lasting, but you go on living all the same. And so people love – in the same way they live – longing for it to last but without any hope of its lasting. They love with their eyes closed and with an uneasiness that permeates their happiness, and they don't think and don't want to think.

The night air creeps in through the closed window. So near to the sky but the stars are dim. In the far distance there is the pale flash of lost lightning and then darkness falls once more, the quiet outpouring of darkness, and gradually, like a mirage, there emerge the outline of the first tower and the soaring chimney, and the plinth for a statue without a statue, and lower and lower. The windows are dark; behind them they are all asleep: those who build the monuments, and those who knock them down, those who light the lights and those who put them out, those who study and those who hate all those who study, those who love each other and those who flee towards love, those who have never known love, and those who betray, and those who flee from betrayal into the arms of pathetic slobs in search of sympathy at least, and those in the stripy clothes and those who watch them, and those who await their arrival with painful anxiety, and those who torture their own love with worrying.

And I'll go down and be like them under the dim light of the street lamps and someone will catch sight of me and say, You're our little sister. You're so alone there. Come with us. And I'll go anywhere, but I'll go – and I'll float and fall, so long as . . . and higher and higher right up to the silhouette of the last tower and the soaring chimney, and the stars, the tiny, enormous stars, and she half closes her eyes, and the stars gradually go out, and instead it is here standing in front of her with its grey coat and long grey mane, the ground dusted with hoar frost, the meadow stretching from horizon to horizon and moving through it is an entire enormous herd of similarly graceful creatures and she is lying in the middle of the meadow and watching and cannot understand how anyone could kill these splendid creatures because of ugly little caged animals and she watches the horses shake their proud heads and can see the enormous herd come closer together and then move apart, and sees them make love – horses – in the middle of the meadow, in the middle of their single day and their single night, with their soft manes, those free horses, lovers for a single night in the middle of a long eternal silent night, and sees a foal running through the herd on spindly legs. My little brothers, she whispers, and no longer feels anxiety. Her tiredness has been soaked up by the hay of the meadow and she is so light that she can fall and float. And thus she sleeps, half undressed, in the rocking chair, while beyond the opening in the roof the day dawns and the foul-smelling city day descends on the room and the free end of the blue twine swings almost imperceptibly to and fro in the invisible draught.

(1964)

24

THE ASSEMBLY LINE

1

What a morning, a totally uncitylike morning, blue sky above the rooftops, a sky like a seascape, wouldn't it be great to be sailing on it, and fields, it'd be great: ever onwards, if only it were possible to go onwards for ever, never land, never disembark, just ever onwards and the sun would go on rising and you as well, don't just stand there gawking, move along and climb aboard, the tram full of heat, the stench of bodies, suddenly his legs went to jelly, because he didn't manage to have a wash, and the day ahead of him – there was still a chance, but only if the workshop collapsed or there was a plague, CLOSED DUE TO PLAGUE, then I'd head off with Ladya, closed due to plague, oh, Jesus, maybe Eva would go too, even though she went and got married, pity, we'd all head off, closed due to plague, there was still a chance today; he dashed towards the gate and from a distance he could make out a white notice, the letters blurred, closed, if only it said closed, but it was only an announcement of a meeting for all staff, he should have known, he spat, the time clock, the mechanical watchdog, the unsmiling watchdog of your life, open your jaws you beast, six-o-four, he dashed past the watchman and across the grey yard full of swirling ash, pushed the door open with his shoulder, workshop number one, past the rumbling presses, Anča cutting tin as usual, it's already given her a back like a hazel stick, like a bow, they should cut you out a hole in the ground, you wouldn't have to bend so much – if I were an engineer . . . but then who'd care about you, another door and he could already see them standing in that never-ending never-changing row, as every month, as on every summer day and every rainy and miserable and snowy day and on the day he died too if only he could come and take a look then: at one end a bald patch at the other end Eva – hair rinsed the colour of a duckling, she's got married, can't be helped – an empty space alongside Ladya, that's mine, one big and three small cogs in the right hand, two small axles in the left, slide them on, let them click into place, test them, then take four screws and screw them into the holes, hang it up, the foreman's standing in for me now, he's not foreman any more, he's me, that's the kind of place it is: whoever turns up (it could be a preacher or a tight-rope walker, a one-legged deaf wrestler; he could have been that morning at his mother's funeral or come from his first time with a girl) that same day would have to take one big and three small cogs in his right hand and reach for the axles with his left. The foreman's gaze was fixed on the hands of the clock, that was something he could do while he was working, everyone could, stare and think, and even think, while the index finger of his right hand fitted the axle exactly into the holes in the casing. The foreman opened his mouth full of greyish porcelain teeth, there's going to be another speech like on television, move off instead, Jesus, it's only six-ten, nine in fact, but it'll soon be ten, while I look at it and the foreman goes on gassing, anyway it's a waste of . . . one big and three small cogs, now he's finished, Marie's wearing a sweater of some kind today, one big cog, it's all hot air anyway, one day he'll come and he won't find me here, believe me, that's one day I'd just love to be here, what bliss, and just to look at his face, except that by then I'll be riding my own horse, four screws, screw them in the holes . . . at last he's . . . and it's peaceful, the conveyor belt moves along quietly, take it off and hang it up, Marie's screwdriver squeaks, six-sixteen, an odd stain on the white wall, a strange bluish blotch. He chased it down a totally white road, through an alley of damp-leaved cherry trees, steam rose from the meadows, hi there! under the trees two fellows jumped up and waved madly.

He stopped.

Sorry, something terrible's happened. He's dead, most likely.

They made him follow them with his motorbike across the field. The tyres became clogged with red clay. He was lying behind a thick hedge. His shirt torn, blood – a fish-shaped knife sticking out of his chest. He leaned over the man. But of course, he assured himself, the blade went straight into the heart. Was he anything to do with you?

No, thank goodness.

He flexed the dead man's elbow, this man must have died just a moment ago, and then he noticed the footprints running directly from there, the narrow footprints of a woman, little indents left by the heels, he kick-started the motor, for a few more moments he could still hear that cry of despair, what could he . . . and he was already dashing off on the trail like a bloodhound. The motor howled up the hill; it's going to suffer again. Now he had to give some thought to where he was actually going, what sort of trail he was following, what he was letting himself in for. He inhaled the deep chill of the forest, a mossy chill, rotting pine needles, slimy roots, pale tree fungi. She stumbled along just ahead of him, still trying to escape. A feeble, desperate attempt. Why are you running away, I might . . . she turned her face to him and he could make out eyes wide with fear – dog-brown eyes.

Was that your . . . ?

No.

Yes, it's okay. I could tell.

He liked the look of her. She was so extremely, so incredibly, beautiful. Whatever had happened for her to . . . He lifted her up cautiously. She had to sit behind him. The touch of her fingers passed through his flanks like drops of warm rain, like kisses and made him shudder. At last it was here, the big moment, at last he could just go on, driving ever onwards, day and night, never stopping, and the low swaying woods rushing past, damp rocks and still the touch of her fingers and her warm breath.

'This is awful shoddy stuff,' Ladya protested. 'Look, this is the third one today.' And he tossed the part into the crate behind him.

'Yeah.'

'I came looking for you yesterday with Libuše. We were going for a swim.'

Six thirty-seven. The first ray of sunlight shot through the window and landed on the table just in front of him.

'It's going to be another scorcher,' said Ladya. 'Can't you

make it today at all? You could bring that girlfriend of yours, that Blanka.'

'I'm not sure.' After all, his yacht was already swaying in the breeze out there in the gulf ready to sail. He was lying with Matt on the green deck: the tom-cat was asleep in the unbearable burning heat of the sun. The water stank. On the nearby shore they were madly dancing the twist and he observed the gyrating couples through his telescope; a white-trousered saxophonist, sailors, girls in almost transparent dresses. They staggered in rhythm. He liked the one in the cherry-red dress: tanned legs and almost-white hair. And her back virtually bare. Would you care to dance?

She shrugged.

I expect she can't understand me, but so what . . . He gestured with his head and she set off after him, down the stone steps and the wooden gangplank across the narrow strip of water separating his boat from the shore. He sent Matt off below deck, started the engine and sat down at the wheel. She was sitting side-on to him, her legs dangling over the side of the boat and almost skimming the green waves and white surf – those naked, tanned legs.

Don't sit there like that! And when she didn't budge he secured the wheel. The smooth, naked, tanned shoulders. She turned her face to him. She moved her lips: where were they heading, or, or . . . There was no reply to that anyway, so instead he said, Babe, you're fantastic, I'm really gone on you, you're like a . . . a . . . He leaned over her and she opened her lips slightly, ever so slightly, the narrowest of gaps, but even so he caught sight of pure whiteness, he continued to grip her shoulders and it suddenly felt as if they were gradually leaning backwards and he leaned over with them and then fell and almost cried out except that it was a light, unbearably light, dizzy fall, he checked himself mid-way, his left hand was already fitting the axle, but his right had let go of the cogs, the conveyor belt had stopped, ten to eight. Marie was still tightening screws, but then she put down her screwdriver, stretched herself slightly and sat down on an upturned crate. 'I feel so . . .' she said.

He wiped his hands on his trousers and moved back several paces to where he had a little three-legged cobbler's stool ready and waiting and pulled a sandwich out of his pocket – he wasn't hungry but he never knew what to do during the first break. The others were sitting around, holding forth. He had never had the gift of the gab and anyway he still couldn't get used to the fact he wasn't an apprentice any more and had the same rights as everyone else; they even turned and talked in his direction too. He sat there on the cobbler's stool, tall and thin, staring at them, chewing slowly.

Then he got up and had to go round the whole conveyor belt, and through the narrow concrete alley between the machines. A layer of dust stuck to the windowpanes but it was still possible to see the narrow yard through them. A few dozen motorbikes stood there, one old chestnut tree was shedding its blossoms, and above the yard, above the dark sooty wall, towered an enormous chimney, and above that the sky, a sky as narrow as the yard. It was still clear blue.

It's going to be another real scorcher. He had just two minutes left. Between this window and the next stood an aquarium on an iron base. Eva stood by it holding a white cardboard cone in her long fingers and her yellow rinse glinted like metal in the sunlight.

'Well,' he strolled over to her, 'how are your whales doing?'

And he watched the translucent fish rush to the surface and snap at the food.

'Be thankful we've got them here.' She had a voice like pond water. She got married only a few weeks ago. She must have hooked him with that voice of hers or maybe it was the effect of that yellow rinse when she's standing with the sun behind her.

The two of them made their way back through the concrete alley between the machines; a pity, if only she hadn't got married . . . He went and stood in his place, taking the one big and three small cogs with his right hand. The axle was already fitted. Then he inserted the four screws, hung it up and took one big and three small cogs in his right hand and two small axles in his left. The loudspeaker on the opposite wall crackled for a moment and made an announcement.

'If only they'd stop that rubbish,' said Ladya, 'and put some proper music on.'

Marie switched off her screwdriver for a moment: 'I wouldn't mind being the one who put the records on, though.'

The voice fell silent; they were playing a polka as it happened to be on top of the pile.

Some dream, he thought to himself, sitting there in an office playing records. Jesus some dream. They're not allowed to play anything decent anyway; people would listen and stop working. 'A fat lot of fun that would be,' he said to Marie, but she was most likely lost in thought again; all she could ever think about was her bloke. That's where he had an advantage: he could leap on to his horse and ride off whenever he wanted to. If it wasn't for that damn music . . . He used to like music and singing, but that loudspeaker with its constant . . . He hated music now, any kind. Luckily he was able to ignore it. So get on, get on, the familiar voice of the doctor shouted at him. What are you waiting for? That woman's at death's door and this is her only hope, and he slipped a small package into the saddle bag. Now he leaped into the saddle and galloped along the dusty path beside the banana plantation, the unrelenting and motionless sun blazing ahead of him, and then the trail came out on to a strange plain of cactuses: tall bulging stems with fat leaves which threw shadows here and there; tiny hummingbirds flew above them and huge butterflies sailed over the bright red flowers. He liked the butterflies, the way they soared, brightly coloured like neon signs. They helped him forget the extreme heat. He laid his head on the horse's neck and closed his eyes slightly so that all he could see now were swirling rainbow-coloured specks, they were the specks of the hummingbirds and the cactus flowers and huge butterflies and he was delighted to be flying through this parched landscape and able to see so many rainbow colours. Then he caught the sound of nearby drums. They were probably part of an incantation against the poison – and what else could they do since he was carrying the only remedy in his saddle bag?

She was lying on a white mattress in a low hut woven from sugar cane. Her skin was very dark and her eyes were already blind.

He took out the syringe. He was still surrounded by people and when he stuck the needle into the dusky arm he could see the liquid slowly disappear from the glass tube.

She'll be better by evening, he announced to the old man who had been standing at his side throughout. They emerged from the hut and the man asked him, How shall I repay you?

He replied, I am merely doing my duty. And in fact he really did not want anything, he was very happy to be able to do what he had done, to ride across the dusty plain and help a woman; if you were able to give her to me, he thought to himself, but said nothing and the man couldn't understand why he refused money, that he was genuinely happy to be doing something he really liked.

'In fact I don't know if we'll be going,' said Ladya.

'Why?'

'It's a drag . . . And then there's the meeting,' he added with annoyance. 'How are you supposed to feel like going anywhere after that?'

'That's a fact,' he said, almost relieved. He now picked up one big and three small cogs with his right hand and two small axles with his left, slid them on, let them click into place, tested them, then took four screws and inserted them into the holes.

Unless you gave me a butterfly, he suggested, a blue butterfly. But his horse was tired and out of breath by now – the butterfly flapped around like a piece of crêpe paper that had torn itself away from some decorations at a village fete; Jesus, it's nine already, forty more minutes to go before the main break: I'll have a pickled herring today and a glass of that black muck – our Coca-Cola. He picked up one big and three small cogs with his right hand and two small axles with his left, gazing all the while at the white wall opposite: it looked like a flour sack, maybe if he breathed out hard enough the bag would collapse and cover him in floury darkness; he closed his eyes slightly and spurred his horse.

He dismounted by an ordinary cliff at the side of the Vltava. Blanka was two paces behind him. They were both trudging along with rucksacks on their backs. Come on, I'll give you a hand, he told her as they started to climb a narrow path in the rocks. But she only snapped at him, Leave off!

There's no need to be so . . . but he felt a pang of regret. Of course he ought to be happy that she had come with him and was now climbing with him up this path that led to a totally deserted forest, but he felt regret instead, because he suspected she was thinking of how to slip away from him, how to shut herself in her tent, keep quiet and act the innocent while he lost his temper because he loved her.

He was definitely quite fond of her and could tell her so if he wanted, except that he never managed to say things like that . . . He let her move ahead of him and all he could see now were her tanned legs and the big rucksack and above it her almost-white hair.

Babe, you're fantastic, it occurred to him. He reached out and said, Come on, I'll give you a hand.

She didn't object, but nor she did utter another word. So they climbed to the top of the slope and the footpath wound through a sparse birch wood.

Listen, she said, why don't do you do something . . . something . . . she could not find the right word, but it seemed she wanted to say: something decent, something classy, a white-collar job, a . . .

What's wrong? he snapped at her. Didn't you see those bikes on the way here?

So what? As if it was you who made them. You . . . she laughed, all you know how to do is stick a couple of cogs into the gear box, apart from that you're totally ham-fisted and useless.

Just like everyone else, he said angrily. But a fat lot you understand with your lacquered head!

She was going to make some comment but he cut her short; And you can pack in all that crap. The last thing I want to do is go on about it here.

But Bohouš, she said.

About my bloody gear boxes, he let fly. I don't need a girl who keeps harping on about things like that.

But Bohouš, she repeated.

It's the last thing I need, he roared at her. Arguing the toss with you about our gear boxes.

But Bohouš! Her voice now gave way and she started to wail like a siren.

'The scorcher is on its way,' Ladya said, wiping his forehead with his sleeve. 'I'd sooner jack it in and head straight for the water.'

'Yeah.'

'When we were at school,' Ladya said, 'there was a whole gang of us. We'd just skive off and be down at the water first thing in the morning.'

'True enough.'

'It's ages ago now – five years already, would you believe?' and as he passed him the box he gave him a sympathetic look as if to say, Pack it in and get the hell out of here, go and make for the water, or just head off somewhere, straight ahead, ever onwards; and he felt an odd sensation in his legs, they were already on their way, running, the tar was a bit sticky underfoot, very sticky; he gulped and blinked his burning eyes. He picked up one big and three small cogs with his right hand and two small axles with his left, slid them on, let them click into place, tested it, then took four screws and inserted them into the holes. His horse was completely tired out and lay exhausted at his feet, nine thirty-five, great, he said to himself, it'll soon be the main break, time will start to fly now, I'll have two Coca-Colas. With Ladya she'd definitely be . . . he was already looking forward to the afternoon, however it turned out. Just so long as that meeting doesn't . . . and he picked up one big and three small cogs with his right hand and two small axles with his left, gazing all the while at the white wall opposite.

2

Outside the hot, dazzling white light hit them. It always filled him with a yearning for distant countries. In the park in front of the factory he caught sight of Libuše still waiting for Ladya, the two whole hours they'd been stuck in that meeting. That was loyalty, all right; nobody hung around for him. They were bound to entreat him to go for a swim, but he was hardly going to play the third . . . so he headed off in the opposite direction.

'Bohouš . . .'

'I haven't got the bike here,' he shouted.

'I'll give you a lift home then. Libuše won't mind waiting here a moment!'

'I can't today!' He wandered along the hot street, just his luck, not a single . . . All the things you could do on a day like this, but what?

At home there was just the tom-cat asleep. Mum and Dad were on the afternoon shift. In the flat the heat hung motionless. He opened a window. 'Had your lunch, Matt?'

In the pantry he found some dumplings soaked in gravy. He stuffed one in his mouth and tossed a piece to the tom-cat. The cat didn't budge, in the heat. It was hot and there was a horrible bland emptiness, on a day like this; he went over to the cupboard and rummaged in the terrible mess until he found the SHIP'S LOG, but pointlessly, really: what sense was there at this moment and on a day like this, even if it was coming to its end? If only one wasn't so totally, so utterly . . . What then? In fact there was only her, he swallowed, she was that day, or the end of it, his swelling hope. The telephone booth beneath his window loomed emptily.

He was scarcely going to beg her, she'll find some excuse anyway, but what else. Otherwise the whole day would just fizzle out if it were allowed to go dry without any moisture.

The moment he stepped into the booth he was drenched in sweat.

'Hello,' came the voice.

'It's me. What are you doing this evening?'

'What else?' said the voice. 'Swotting as usual.'

'What?'

'Everything.'

He fell silent. It was impossible to breathe in the booth. He should have gone to the river.

'And what about you?' said the voice.

'Nothing.'

'Lucky you.'

He wiped his forehead. 'You won't spend the whole time at it, though.'

'I can't say.'

'You'll have done enough by this evening, won't you?'

'I can't say,' she repeated.

'I'll wait for you then. Near your place by the cinema. What time?'

'I don't know.'

'Seven then,' he decided. 'Will you come?'

'Maybe . . .'

'Bye, then.'

'Ciao.'

He went back home. This time he opened the ship's log and wrote: 20th May: longitude 158° 13′ 27″ W., latitude 30° 5′ 16″ S., sea calm, a hot windless day. A bit boring as before. Matt still sleeping. Holding course for the Friendly Isles. Four sharks to port. I'm already looking forward to this evening.

Then he remembered: There's only a few days' supply of drinking water left, but we've not lost hope.

He realized he was thirsty. He put the ship's log away again. The beer in the pantry was like coffee. Then he took out the disassembled radio and gazed into the jumble of wires for a long time without moving. Nothing gave him pleasure lately: not even reading or repairing. He didn't even particularly enjoy going swimming – everything seemed the same and everything was over so quickly, he had nothing to look forward to. Except her, a little. He liked her, even though he wasn't sure where he stood, or maybe exactly because he didn't.

He abandoned the radio; there's time enough for that at the rate I'm going. He couldn't work out why he was so fed up lately. Well, actually he didn't think about it too much, he just felt it, like a weariness: in his legs, in his head, in his hands and in front of his eyes.

There were some people who were capable of putting up with anything: whether or not they won the lottery, or their side lost last Sunday . . . if they arrived a minute late that morning . . . if they had a row with the foreman. He couldn't understand them, though they were probably better off than him. He strolled along the street – silent families going home, the smell of their dinner from the windows. He tried to think about Blanka, what he'd talk to her about. But he couldn't think of anything. Nothing at all. Nothing had happened today or yesterday, apart from the fact he arrived four minutes late for work – but he could hardly talk to her about . . .

He arrived five minutes early. He stood at the corner and leaned against a red and yellow railing. Two houses away there was a single-storey suburban cinema. The red neon sign paled in the setting sun. There was no one around, it must be in the middle of the film. In a window opposite a woman was walking around in her slip, but she was no longer young. The big green clock on the corner – someone had broken the glass with a stone and knocked off the minute hand, but the hour hand showed between eleven and twelve. He felt the urge to knock the hour hand off too and looked round for a stone, but couldn't find one . . . it's seven o'clock anyway. If she didn't come this time he'd send her to . . . but it was only one minute past seven. In fact he began to miss her; if they were to start going out together for real, then in the summer they could all – Ladya, Libuše and the two of them – go off somewhere camping maybe. It would make a great fortnight. Ten past seven. He found the wait exhausting. When she comes, if she comes, he'd say something to her, but what then? He didn't fancy the cinema; if she weren't so stubborn it would be easy to go somewhere out of town; just a few streets away and you were in the scrub; there was somewhere there for lying down and everything else; he knew where it was – when they were still in eighth class a whole gang of them would go out and flash lamps – the guys would go mad – once a guy knocked out one of his teeth. Seven-fifteen. He spat. He walked past the broken clock and slouched along the footpath to the ugly blocks of flats.

Buzzers on a grubby board.

'Yes?' asked the rusty interphone.

'It's me. What's the problem?'

'Is that you?'

'Who else would it be?' he said. 'You promised me . . .'

'"Maybe",' the perforated metal corrected him. 'Actually I said I wasn't sure. I told you about all the cramming I've got to do. You don't know how lucky you are.'

'Yeah,' he said, 'not half.'

'You could come upstairs for a moment,' said the metal, 'though I don't know about my parents.'

'Bye, then. I'm not waiting any longer tonight.'

'Ciao, then.'

'Or tomorrow,' he added.

'Ciao.'

'Or ever again,' he concluded. But the rusty metal had fallen silent.

It wouldn't be night for a good while yet; he was hardly going to go home to bed. He didn't fancy going to find the other one either, not today anyway. Sometimes he used to look her up, but not today. He hadn't given her a thought the entire day, he'd had no desire to, in fact; so why this evening?

I should have taken my bike and gone to the river with Ladya, he thought as he sloped off towards the tram stop, there's always some fun by the river, and girls, and failing that there's sun and sand, sun and sand, someone playing a guitar, coloured swimsuits. He reached the main street. Wax dummies smiled out of shop windows. He gawked at them for a moment before getting on a tram. Jesus, but seeing . . . The tram car was empty except for some old bird and her dog; out that late and with a dog too, the old bird; if only she, if only, there's nothing wrong with her, but I don't . . . I ought to get off. The rails screeched wearily. He was falling into a dark sack. He should have gone to the river with Ladya instead. Ladya's a . . . those tricks of his, like yesterday when he told the foreman, when he told the foreman . . . he chuckled quietly. This summer we could take our rucksacks and head off somewhere together. If he wanted to take Libuše, though, I'd have to . . .

He got off the tram. The light from the dirty café lit the street – the Morning Star. What creep dreamed up that name for it. He went inside. There were three guys drinking beer. No one behind the counter. He leaned against it and waited.

Eventually she came out. In extremely grubby overalls. Small and thin, her cheeks grey after a long day. Her lipstick was almost all rubbed off. She caught sight of him and smiled wearily. Two gold teeth shone in her mouth. 'Is that you Bohouš?'

'Who else?'

'Come to see me?'

He leaned on the counter. His gaze was fixed on her face but he said nothing and gave nothing away.

So she said, 'I'm really tired today.'

'Yeah, it's evening already.'

She looked at the clock. 'I close up in another twenty minutes.'

'I'll wait for you!'

'I don't know . . . I'm awful . . . It's really nice of you to come, but I'm completely fagged out.'

'You'll perk up outside.'

'I don't think so. Not today. Do you want something?'

'Let me have a beer.'

She poured him a beer and he stared at her breasts beneath the grubby overalls. She was older than him, but not much, maybe only five years; he'd never asked her, maybe not so

41

much – girls soon went to seed in this job. She wasn't especially plain, apart from those gold teeth and her nose, but she'd never been his idea of . . .

'Fancy something to eat? There's not much left anyway.' The last open sandwiches were going dry under the glass. She put two of them on a plate for him.

'It's the heat that does it,' she said. She smoothed her hair slightly and looked at him.

He took the beer and the sandwiches over to a table. The last of the three drinkers finished his beer and they left; just the two of them remained.

'Bohouš,' she said, coming over to him, 'you really oughtn't wait for me. It's nice of you, but I'm dreadfully tired today.'

'It doesn't matter. I'll wait.'

'It's up to you . . . Would you pass me those glasses?'

He stood up and brought her the glasses the three had left. She rinsed them under the tap and stood them alongside the others. 'I shouldn't think there'll be anyone else in now,' she said. 'It wouldn't be worth their while.' She poured herself a beer and sat down with him at the table. 'So what were you doing today?'

'You know,' he mumbled. 'I was supposed to be going for a swim but it didn't work out.'

'Someone diddled me again today,' she said, slowly. 'I don't see how it could have happened.'

She fixed a tired gaze on him and her arm lay wearily on the table top: a small hand, the veins showing through coarse skin; her nail varnish had cracked during the day. He covered her hand with his own. She didn't move a muscle but just kept staring into his face, or beyond it, somewhere behind him. Then she raised her glass and finished her beer. 'I don't see how it

42

could have happened,' she repeated. 'I suppose I must have miscounted when I was giving that tram bloke his change.'

'Which bloke?' he asked and took two ten-crown notes out of his wallet.

'Forget it,' she said. 'Just forget it.'

He left the money on the table. 'There was one guy today,' she began to tell him, 'with a sort of a limp. I see him in here occasionally. He got drunk and kept going on about being falsely convicted or something. It seems he went to jail,' she went on slowly, 'and got out last year, before Christmas. But what does he have to keep thinking about it for? There's no point thinking about it the whole time.' She took his glass and her own and stood them on the counter. Then she went to the door and pulled down the grill.

She let him out the back way.

'Well, then?' he asked.

''Fraid not.'

Her house stood at the end of a dark street. If only she weren't so tired. Just a little further. Go dancing, at least. If only she weren't so tired. 'Can you smell that?' he said. There was the scent of something but he couldn't tell what. She unlocked the door. 'You must have an early start tomorrow too . . .'

'I know.'

He followed her down a long row of doors. She lived in a single room; water dripped quietly in the passage. 'I'll have to mend that for you,' he said.

'You've been promising that . . . Ever since you first came . . .'

She started making up the bed on the couch. The place was empty apart from a cupboard, a small table, a chair and the couch. And two pictures on the wall: some sort of cliff above a river and a birch wood. He sat down and waited.

'Why don't you have a wash in the meantime?' she asked.

'Okay.' He went out into the passage. Hair grips, a bottle of egg shampoo, lipstick and a few half-squeezed tubes lay scattered on the shelf by the sink. He ran some water before taking off his shirt.

'There was a bloke I knew once . . .' she called. 'You don't mind me talking about them?'

'No!' he said, over the sound of the water.

'There's no point, though.' He heard her slapping the eiderdown. 'I'm completely fagged out today,' she called. 'Should I make some coffee?'

She opened the door slightly and he could see the kettle in her hand. 'Fill it for me.'

He had finished washing long ago, but he stayed there splashing himself with the cold water.

'He used to drink an awful lot of coffee,' she remembered, 'that bloke. He'd drink four coffees of an evening. Big ones, and I used to have to make them with three spoonfuls of coffee. He'd always bring it with him. He was a doctor. They posted him to somewhere in the country where he was all on his own. And had to make night calls too. He used to before . . . and he said he had got used to it. So he couldn't get to sleep,' she said. 'Some nights he didn't manage to fall asleep at all.'

He dried himself with a soft, fragrant towel. 'You told me before.'

'About that bloke?'

'About him driving to see that woman who was dying.'

'There you go,' she said, 'I'd completely forgotten.'

'What's he doing now?'

'Him? No idea. He hasn't shown up in ages. Some of them

disappear all of a sudden. They don't even try to get in touch . . . As if we hadn't been . . . You won't, will you?'

'Of course I won't,' he muttered.

'Maybe that coffee did for him,' she said quickly, 'and that's why he's not been in touch.'

They were sitting opposite each other – he by now only in his boxer shorts – and drinking coffee. 'Come to bed,' he said. 'Seeing you're so tired.'

'All right.'

He knew she would now spend ages washing herself. He hated waiting for her to finish washing, the time he had to stay in the room alone. It wasn't an ugly room, just empty and alien. There was nothing out of the ordinary, not even a spot on the wall, not even an old radio, or an aquarium with a single blue fish.

'Why the silence?' she called.

'I don't feel like talking!' Now he too felt an oppressive weariness. He always did lying here under a strange eiderdown, when he knew he ought to say something: to say he loved her and why he had come, or about the way things were and were going to be. Or at least to think about her and look forward to her. But weariness would force him to close his eyes, and he would start to fall into the dark sack with coarse sides, always the same material; it enveloped him and didn't let in the tiniest ray of light, or thought or image, even. He lay there totally still until suddenly he noticed that the coarse-woven side of the bag, the dark impervious material, was moving, slowly, inch by inch, moving almost imperceptibly: an endless grey conveyor belt.

A few quiet footsteps, the click of the light switch and he felt her body at his side. 'My little boy,' she said, 'my pet. Did you fall asleep?'

He opened his eyes, and a bright reflection moved across the ceiling before her face got in the way: two big shining . . .

'Now I'm glad you're here,' she whispered. 'I'm always glad when you're with me.'

She waited in case he said something too, but she knew he'd probably stay silent. He never said anything. Sometimes it made her sad. 'My daddy-long-legs,' she whispered, 'my horrible daddy-long-legs.' Then she touched his chin with her lips, then his neck, breathing quickly and loudly, then his cheeks. Then she moved her lips to his, put her arms around him. And this was the moment, the moment that always made him come back for more. He knew it, she knew it. The soft pressure of her body. He was falling. He could feel himself gently floating. The unbearably light, dizzy fall, now it was for real . . . Completely and totally happy at this moment. Nothing could equal this moment. Nothing tempted him away from it, everything converged here in this single instant, even though it was so brief and then after there would just be an ordinary old night.

'My little boy,' she whispered afterwards. She waited but he only breathed wearily. 'Do you like it here with me?' she asked.

'Yeah,' he whispered. He tried to hold onto the moment but didn't know how, and felt that even now it was beginning to slip away from him and he was beginning to fall into the night. The woman next to him moved slightly, whispered something, got up and pattered out to the passage. Water splashed noisily into the sink. She returned with a grey washbasin and a towel over her naked shoulder. She put the basin on the chair. 'Don't you want to wash yourself?'

So he had to get up and wash himself while she lay behind him. 'I don't know if I feel like sleeping any more,' she whispered. 'What if I switched on the radio?'

46

Then they lay side by side and the radio cast a dark rhomboid against the wall.

'Aren't you hungry?' she asked.

'No.'

'You usually . . .' she started. 'My little boy,' she whispered, 'do you love me a little?'

He said nothing. A horribly sweet tune issued from the radio. Just as well he was able to ignore it. The motionless rhomboid. The cold strangeness of this room, of this night, this music, these words, this loving; he half closed his eyes and tried to conjure up his horse, quietly clicking his tongue at it, but couldn't even hear a response, it was sleeping somewhere – maybe his horse was worn out by that long day, wearily staring into a night full of stars while his warm nostrils quivered. The world was falling into a dark sack, the same old material. He lay there motionless: if only something, something were to come – a white horse at the corner of the street, Morning Star, something . . .

'Bohouš!' she shook him. 'Bohouš, it's time you were gone.'

He leapt up. The grey washbasin was still standing on the chair. The low, cold sun shone into the room . . .

'There's bread in the cupboard . . . And some kind of almond pieces,' she said sleepily.

'I haven't got time,' he said testily. But he opened the cupboard and quickly cut a slice of bread.

'Will you come again this evening?' she asked when he was dressed.

'Don't know . . . Maybe I'll go somewhere with Ladya.'

'Do come,' she said. 'I know you will anyway.'

The trams were stiflingly full and his legs were weak from lack of sleep. He hadn't even managed to wash . . .

★

The time clock, the unsmiling watchdog of your days. Six-ten, there'd be words again. He dashed past the watchman and across the grey yard full of swirling ash. Workshop number one, past the rumbling presses, Anča cutting tin as usual, one more door and he could already see them in that never-ending never-changing row . . . one big and three small cogs in the right hand, two small axles in the left, slide them on, let them click into place, test them, then take four screws and screw them into the holes, hang it up.

The foreman's gaze was fixed on the clock: six-fifteen. Jesus it's only six-fifteen. He grabbed one big and three small cogs in his right hand, two small axles in the left. He fitted them. Then he took four screws and put them in the holes. He passed the first box on to Marie. She turned to him and smiled slightly. The foreman's getting fed up; there'll be a bit of peace at last. The conveyor belt moved quietly. Take it off, hang it up. Marie's screwdriver squeaked. He could hear the clip-clop of hooves. He cantered along a totally white road through an alley of cherry trees with damp leaves. Steam rose from the meadows.

(1963)

LINGULA

1

The student canteen was a long, bleak hall in the basement and its walls, apart from the glass one at the back, had blind alcoves instead of windows. The canteen committee, it is true, had added some hand-painted commandments in an effort to conceal its drabness,

NO SPILLING OF FOOD! NO LEAVING OF DIRTY
CROCKERY! NO SMOKING!

However they did little to cheer the place up and Tomáš and his friends used to carry their lunches to the glass wall. It was airier there and brighter and the table under the tenth commandment had one short leg and nobody sat there, so it was the perfect place for dumping coats, briefcases and empty soup dishes.

They got used to the spot – the last table in the second row – and cut a large scorpion out of cardboard, writing on it the words,

BIOLOGY – RESERVED!

Just beyond the glass wall lay a small garden: two lilac bushes, a low acacia bush, a white magnolia and a forsythia. Blackbirds and a pair of turtle-doves nested there. The students paid little attention to it, simply tossing their leftovers to the birds in the winter, and one day were almost surprised to find that the acacia was putting out its first leaves just as they were studying the *viciaceae* family.

When the lilac was starting to bloom they arrived to find an unknown girl sitting at the table with the short leg. Her hair was almost white and combed into a beehive. Her eyes were olive-green beneath dark brows and her neck was long. She sat as erect as a statue and held her knife and fork with such elegance that she could have been sitting in the Hotel International, or on a film set.

They did not take their eyes off her the entire time she was eating while she spared them not a single glance, as though unaware of anyone sitting nearby, or of the tenth commandment above her head that read,

BE CONSIDERATE TO YOUR COMRADES!

When she finished her meal she wiped her mouth on her handkerchief while gazing blankly into the distance. Then she got up and looked around briefly. She couldn't help noticing them now, but she made no sign and left, walking away from them in her stiletto-heeled shoes, with the short, quick steps of the ideal secretary.

They stayed at lunch longer than usual, droning on about the girl: her legs, her hips, her breasts, her eyes. They couldn't just let her disappear like that. Tomáš was at the time the only one of them to have any free moments, so the task fell to him, even though the general opinion was that it was probably beyond him. The next day they caught sight of her from a distance. She was sitting at the same table. Opposite her was some guy at least fifteen years her senior – balding, stylish little spectacles perched on his snub nose, one corner of his shirt collar turned up.

She was eating like a duchess. He slurped his soup noisily, his face almost in the soup bowl.

'Do you like it?' they heard him ask.

'Yes.'

For a long time the two of them said nothing and then she asked, 'How about you?'

'Of course – I'm here with you!' He stopped eating and bared his brownish teeth.

'Stop it – I don't like that sort of talk.' They ate the rest of the meal in silence. Then he took away the dirty plates while everyone congratulated Tomáš because against someone like that he was in with a chance.

Over the next two days they found out that the fellow lectured in family law, was divorced and had a two-tone Škoda Spartak, but about her they discovered nothing. Nobody knew her or had seen her before. Apparently she wasn't a student but simply attached to the lawyer, and after that first day had only appeared in his company.

Soon they got used to her and stopped listening to what the

pair at the next table were saying. They were almost always silent anyway – he was still as unappealing and she as perfect as ever; when they finished eating he would clear away the dirty plates and she would remain seated a few moments gazing blankly after him. Then she would follow him and they would go upstairs, holding hands.

She was dubbed 'Tomáš's girl' with friendly mockery: she had been assigned to him and he assigned her to himself too, even though he'd yet to say a word to her. The problem was that fellow didn't budge from her side and she never gave Tomáš a chance to speak to her. By now nobody even expected him to try. Only he thought about it, imagining the moment when he would do it. And since that was so easy to imagine he also imagined the moments that would follow: the two of them sitting together on the terrace of the Brussels Restaurant – music, the midnight dance floor, her olive green eyes, her full lips, kissing her as they danced, then beneath the bridge on the quay, and then in the entrance of the house where she lived, inside, kissing her as she sat on some unfamiliar fine-legged chair, and then making love on an unfamiliar couch – a long, lingering moment. Then he would start all over again.

'What are you doing this afternoon? Do you know you *could* spend it in the company of a fascinating man . . .' No, that wouldn't work. She wouldn't even respond. He stared at his textbook. The *fasciola* and *opisthorchis* genus: heart-shaped bodies with two suckers . . .

'You must be made from the foam of the sea. Let me look at you for a moment. Just a single moment! Just gaze!' She would hardly refuse. But it would look as though he were totally infatuated with her.

'You have a head like a hoopoe.'

'Like a what?'

'Hoopoe!'

A slightly bewildered laugh.

'It's a bird. With a magnificent head. Though nothing to compare with yours!' That sounded promising.

The term's lectures were finished and they no longer all went to lunch together. Some days they didn't set foot outside the student residence but lived on bread and tinned cod in tomato sauce, with poppy-seed buns and potted mushrooms from their mothers, while chatting away about the four features of the dialectic, the unfortunate Belinda Lee, the latest show at the Semafor, about how Fuchs yelled so loudly the last time he failed his annual exams that the cleaning woman on the floor below dropped a jar containing a rare specimen of Chinese crab and the crab and the alcohol skidded over the floor as if alive and the old dear nearly had a heart attack.

Then there was only a day and a night left before the exam. Mulling things over, they revised worms in their heads – he had just got to the order of brachiopods, stupid little sea worms he'd probably never lay eyes on. Maybe today of all days she had come on her own – it would make a wonderful change from these wretched worms! But on the day before the exam?

He thought he might shave, at least. Then he polished his shoes. After all, the canteen was only twenty minutes away. He put on a new shirt – the latest style. He looked quite interesting (he might just borrow a silver cigarette-lighter), he'd enough money, a full hundred crowns he'd been saving for emergencies.

The day was unbearably hot, and the crowded tram was sweaty. He cursed all the idiots around him and resolved that if he actually managed to catch her he would speak to her, even if the dean himself was sitting at the same table.

He saw her from afar – her bright green blouse, the light blond hair. She was sitting at the wobbly table, and the chair opposite was empty.

He quickly collected a lunch and made his way over to her with his plate.

In her low neck-line hung a decorative coin on a bronze chain; her skin was smooth, so fine and smooth. 'Is this place free?'

She looked up in surprise. 'Watch out,' she said. 'You're spilling your soup.'

He tried to match her table manners, but she had had a head start and two dumplings remained on his plate when she finished her meal. There was no time to waste. 'On your own today?' What a daft thing to say. How utterly trivial. 'I suppose he's examining,' he added quickly.

'I've no idea.' She stacked her plates and stood up.

'Wait,' he blurted out. 'What would you say to an afternoon stroll?'

'A what?'

'What else are you doing this afternoon?'

'Going fishing.'

'That's no fun.'

'What do you suggest?'

'Something you've never experienced before. An original and unforgettable evening!'

'You were talking about the afternoon a moment ago.' She picked up the plates with one hand and her handbag with the other and walked away – those short, brisk steps of the ideal secretary.

He hurried after her, up the staircase and then along the hot, overcrowded street. This chance would never come again. He tried desperately to come up with something clever, witty and slightly ironic to say, something charmingly self-assured – but remained silent.

The lights at the intersection were red. 'Well,' she said with her eyes fixed on the red light, 'will we be going in the same direction for much longer?'

'For ever,' he said, despairingly, 'unless you want to destroy me utterly!'

They crossed the intersection, a taxi appeared from the direction of the Powder Tower. She hailed it resolutely.

The driver leaned over the front seat lazily and half opened the back door.

He dashed to hold it open from outside.

'Where to?' asked the man behind the wheel as she got in.

'The Golden Well,' he said, then quickly jumped in and the taxi drove off.

Tight-lipped, she stared ahead. He now caught a slight scent of lilac and was overjoyed: it must have worked. Action is always better than blathering.

The car crossed the river, turning several times into ever narrower streets. 'Sixteen crowns!' declared the driver and quickly cleared the meter.

'Thanks for the lift,' she said. 'Your cheek really is something extraordinary!'

He felt flattered. 'So come on up! There's no point hanging about down here.'

'A truly unusual afternoon,' she said, scornfully. 'Sitting on a terrace and gawking at our city's famous "hundred towers". And a glass of wine with you into the bargain! Was that the best you could dream up?'

'I would have dreamt up something better, but you didn't give me enough time.'

'Well you have plenty now.'

'Okay, I'll think up something original. But let's go and sit on the terrace first.'

After they had climbed the 160 steps he called over the waiter and coolly ordered a bottle of champagne – I'll find out what it tastes like, at least.

The city was truly beautiful. Some of the windows shone like flame and small, old-fashioned tram cars moved soundlessly along the distant embankment. The familiar towers soared upwards and a haze of smoke and exhaust fumes hung over everything.

'We could introduce ourselves,' he suggested.

'Such an incredibly original gambit,' she said. 'My name's none of your business. And yours doesn't interest me in the least.'

He raised his glass, determined not to be put off. 'You're extraordinary. Really extraordinary. And fascinating.'

She looked past him and over the low railing at the dark, sooty roofs. 'And now tell me what you really want.'

'I told you. To spend the afternoon and the evening with you!'

'What would be the point?'

'I don't know . . . We could both be happy, perhaps.'

'You can stop that kind of talk. I've heard it too many times.'

'Won't you tell me something about yourself?'

'No!'

'Are you a student?'

She remained silent.

'Do you love him?'

'Stop it!'

'You're not happy, are you?'

'You say the same thing to every girl and she's amazed you could possibly know. Is that it?'

'But you're not. I can tell!'

'You can stop talking like that immediately – or I'll leave you to sit here on your own.'

He paid for the wine. The tip alone would have bought three lunches at the canteen. He had scarcely forty crowns left.

'Now I hope you'll let me go,' she said at the bottom of the steps. But the question already contained the answer. After all, there was nothing to stop her leaving, there was no need to ask him. Now was the moment to come up with some brilliant subject. Or an anecdote. But he had spent the last days deep in worms.

'I won't,' he said perfunctorily. Last winter he had almost perished in the mountains. Well, that was a bit of an exaggeration, but it had been quite an experience anyway. How could he tactfully steer the conversation towards winter? In the meantime he asked, 'Do you go to the Semafor?'

'As if you cared.'

'That's real modern music. It manages to cheer you up, even when you know the next moment could be your last.' How was that for an ace conversational move! He glanced in her direction but her expression showed no trace of interest.

So he started to describe the dreadful fog, the howling storm, the ice crystals whipping into his face, his breath freezing at his lips.

She walked beside him, indifferent, concentrating on where she was placing her feet and staring straight ahead. It was four in the afternoon and the streets were starting to fill with people who swarmed into shops, hot and sweaty, gaping at shop windows, and barging into him. The queue in front of the ice-cream shop grew longer. Few things could seem as senseless at that moment as a howling storm, snow drifts and the danger of the mountains.

He swallowed repeatedly in desperation as he tried to find a creditable way out of his bind. He described his feelings of total exhaustion.

Some actress or other grinned at him from a poster. Behind her a red car was hurtling into an abyss. He had no idea what kind of film it was, but the poster promised an Italian comedy, so he told her he'd heard it was supposed to be splendid.

She sneered slightly and he dashed off to buy tickets. The film had started long before, but fortunately this particular film didn't seem to need any beginning. He couldn't concentrate at all but tried to pretend he was enjoying himself, laughing loudly at the silliest jokes and looking round at her triumphantly. But she wasn't laughing. Her face was oddly taut, her eyes were barely open, obviously registering nothing, and her mouth seemed to indicate she was in some kind of distress.

There's something strange about her, he said to himself. Maybe something has happened to her. Something I haven't a clue about. Or to him maybe. That's why he didn't come to lunch and the whole time she's been thinking about him. Some tragedy, he decided, that could be quite interesting. It'll be a long while before she's able to confide in me. We were still strangers yesterday but you can count on me!

But it would call for some action, of course.

But what sort of action could one possibly come up with in this absurd world?

Short of taking the tram to Šarka, he thought to himself

peevishly, and throwing myself off the cliff. As proof of my love. Or chucking myself in the Vltava fully clothed. On the other hand, he thought, maybe I'll make do with an ordinary bench and the sort of things that people don't usually talk about. Such as the first time I fell in love, or how I discovered Dad was avoiding Mum, or how they bombed Prague when I was six months old. The house next door was hit. Can you believe it? I could have ceased to exist. If it had fallen a bit closer there could be an empty space sitting next to you.

The film ended.

'It was a bit tedious,' he admitted. 'I'm sorry if you found it boring.'

'Why?' she said in surprise. 'Have you got something even worse up your sleeve?'

'Like?'

'Dancing,' she said. 'That's the next invitation, isn't it? Dinner followed by dancing. I reckon you're the Shooters' Island type. You're not classy enough for the Café Vltava and they don't serve alcohol at the Luxor. You'd be hard pressed to look even slightly debauched there. And at the Fučík Park they only have oompah.'

A suicidal notion took hold of him. 'But that's precisely where I wanted to take you.'

'Aha, you're starting to be original.' She's bound never to have set foot in the place and be horrified of parks and daddies taking time out with their kiddies. 'I'm sure it'll be unforget-table,' she said. 'Will you buy me a balloon and some candy-floss?'

'Whatever you fancy!' He had only been there once himself and had a vague memory of hordes of people and unrelieved boredom. There's nothing more tedious than organized fun.

YOU ARE REQUIRED TO ENJOY YOURSELF! But maybe he'd find something there, something he could use as a starting point! An exhibition of artificial flowers, perhaps. Or a poetry evening. Do you like Holub? Or Morgenstern? Do you know the one about the worm?

Hidden in its shell
A most peculiar worm did dwell

Do you know how the *eunice viridis* procreates? Ugh!

They got on a tram and he bought tickets. He had 16 crowns 40 hellers left.

The park gates were wide open and a man and woman emerged, tottering towards them. She had rumpled clothes and painted lips. Water flowed quietly from the beaks of china dabchicks. They veered to the right and circled the locked sports hall. Trampled paper cups lay scattered in front of empty stalls and a solitary sweeper was piling them into an untidy heap. As they passed, he looked up and nodded in the direction of the empty park benches lining the flower beds. 'Things aren't what they used to be. The lovers are all sitting at home watching telly.'

He was grateful for 'the lovers.' 'Not all of them, as you see.'

'Come on,' she urged, impatiently. 'There has to be something here somewhere!'

There was a new layer of sand on the path and the dark buildings slumbered with their windows forbiddingly shuttered; the empty arena with its banks of seats, the amphitheatre and the great circular structure of the Circlorama. An abstract sculpture of shiny metal rose out of the grass.

He stopped in front of it.

'Anything but that,' she said quickly. 'I don't want to talk about modern art. I'm not interested in Miró or Klee. They don't concern me in the slightest.'

She turned towards him. Her hair shone red in the reflection of the setting sun. She was extremely beautiful at that moment and he forgot what he had intended to say. All he could think was that they might love each other.

'And what does concern you?' he asked.

'Come on,' she said, 'there *must* be something happening here somewhere.'

'There's nothing happening here . . . So what does concern you?'

'Not you, for sure,' she snapped, 'as you have to keep on asking.'

'But you concern *me*! Because I love you.'

'Stop it! Stop that talk!'

'I've had a couple of girlfriends. One of them I really loved.'

'So what?'

'She left me . . . She was my first. I thought I'd never love anyone as much again. But I'll love you more.'

From a long way off came the sound of a brass band, the rattle of goods trucks at the railway station and the clang of a tram car. The sounds only deepened the silence. And the two of them were quite alone in this immense cemetery of entertainment.

He stopped by one of the park benches. 'Shall we sit down?'

She placed her handbag between them and tried to pull her skirt down over her knees.

'I'm serious,' he said.

She stroked the leather of her bag and touched his hand in the process, maybe intentionally. If he hesitated now she would be bound to think he was a beginner; he closed his hand over her fingers. He felt a momentary thrill at the touch. If she doesn't take her hand away, I'll put my arm around her. The thrill grew more intense while deeper inside lurked the fear that it had all been too easy, that she wasn't so remarkable, inaccessible or refined after all, that she could be sitting here with anyone, that she was the same as the rest of them.

She withdrew her hand and placed both hands on her knees without looking at him. Her breath came slowly and calmly. He looked into her face; her features were no longer taut, just very tired.

'Is nothing ever going to happen?' she asked.

'What kind of thing?'

'Something big. Some movement. Will there never be any more revolutions?'

'Revolutions? But we had one!'

'That's not the sort I meant,' she said testily.

'What sort then?'

'Movement of some kind! Hue and cry. A theatre performance on an enormous staircase. In the open air.'

'And that's all?'

'No.' For a moment she spoke as though reciting from some strange text. 'You could do whatever you liked. Join in the play – or not. Or play something else. Walk down that staircase and say nothing and take no notice of anything.'

He didn't understand her. Perhaps she wasn't able to say precisely what she wanted; it was something one had to accept with women. But there was an excitingly wistful note in her voice that he understood. At this moment she seemed extremely close to him.

'What am I to call you?'

'What? Oh, that again . . . Will you stop!'

'But I have to have to call you something!'

'So make something up.' Once more she was totally and haughtily impassive.

Rancour overwhelmed him. 'Okay. I've thought of one. How about Lingula.'

'What?'

'Lingula!'

'If you like,' she said, unconcerned.

A train moved along the embankment. She stared after it. Sparks and light from the windows. He noticed. 'Lingula,' he said, 'there's a station not far from here. We'll take a train.'

'Where?'

'Who cares? . . . It's movement.'

She shrugged.

They got up and walked back along the deserted path. I've only got 16 crowns left, he realized. But we'll always manage to get home if we want to.

No one was waiting at the booking office window. He tipped all his money out on the counter. 'Two eight-crown-twenty tickets,' he said.

'What?'

He caught sight of a spinsterish face and a bewildered look behind dark-framed spectacles.

'Two eight-crown-twenty tickets,' he repeated.

'Where to?'

'It doesn't matter,' he said. 'On the next train.'

'You don't know where you're going?'

'No!'

'There's no such ticket,' the booking-office lady declared. 'You can have one for seven-eighty or eight-forty.'

She passed him two cardboard tickets. 'Hurry up. Your train leaves in four minutes.'

2

The carriage swayed gently and the night flowed past the window. There were four workmen in the compartment, three playing cards while the fourth sat opposite her, watching her in silence and smoking.

She couldn't remember the last time she'd taken the train. Her recent boyfriends had always had cars. And always Spartaks. She'd liked the last one most of all – two-tone, red with a black roof. But apart from that he was the same as the rest, the same talk; a drive to the dam every Saturday – a divorcee. She wasn't even really sure why she went with them. All those cabins on steep slopes. They were stifling hot inside, long into the night. But she had to survive the weekends somehow. She always managed to find someone. If only he hadn't gone on the way he had, though. He was just an ordinary lawyer but with a passion for lyrical verse. Sweetheart, you have eyes like a goldfish and a head like a Madonna, I'd like to take you away with me – or just a little bit of you to put under the glass of my desktop. Those words would come back to her even in the dead of night when all was silent and she was trying desperately to get to sleep. The words would choke her and she would long for the morning to come. She longed for it so much that she would start to whisper out loud, 'Dear God, if only it was morning!'

This student she was travelling with had been telling her stories about some crazy professor or other while the workman kept on looking at her. She looked at him too, but not at his face: he had a thin sinewy neck like a strange landscape of rounded slopes and hollows. In one of the hollows lay a small seashell on a fine chain.

She found it odd that he should wear such a trifle. Perhaps he had been at the seaside and wanted people to know it.

He saw she was watching him and smiled slightly. She smiled too. Just as long as he doesn't start to talk, she thought. She didn't want to hear any talk. About herself, or him or about life.

The train would stop and set off again and there would be the tramp of feet in the corridor. From time to time she could not help laughing at the stories. The workman stared at her intently: perhaps he had stood like that on the seashore, motionlessly scanning the waves, maybe that's why he brought back that seashell, because he loved the sea and wanted to remember it. For a moment she glanced into his calm eyes and she realized that in fact he was unaware of her, he was just staring, looking at the sea or his daughter or some long lost object which he could see only through her.

She smiled at him again. Maybe it wasn't even a smile but an expression of satisfaction.

The train started to brake. The workmen got up and the one opposite her put on his beret and nodded in her direction like an old acquaintance and she replied bye in a tone she kept reserved for her friends.

Now she was alone in the compartment except for that student. He sat opposite her with a sullen look on his face – like Belmondo. He had full lips too, and a straight nose. All he lacked was a bit of carnality.

'You haven't listened to a word I've been saying,' he said, trying to look exasperated. 'Did you know that guy?'

'Yes.' His eyes had none of that man's serenity. She began to feel regret. Whatever possessed me? Where am I going? I don't even know where we'll sleep. But in the end that doesn't matter. So long as there's running water. And he doesn't start talking drivel beforehand.

He's giving me a sheepish look. Why?

He's still only a boy, she realized. He must be younger than me. He's just putting it on. Maybe he'll still manage to like me, it occurred to her. But what's the point, she rebuked herself. Why start all over again? It's of no importance. Nothing's important really. So long as it's nice, a bit nice, at least. From beneath half-closed eyelids she could make out yellowish lights passing the window. 'Come on,' she heard him say. 'We have to get off here.'

It was a small station. Four lamps and beneath them tubs of pelargoniums and a sleepy stationmaster.

'Do you know this place?'

'Not in the slightest.'

They followed the other people along a beaten path in the dark and arrived at a number of lights, one of which belonged to a pub.

'Aren't you going to invite me to dinner?' she asked.

'Naturally,' he said. But he stood outside the door with a look of despair. Finally she recalled how he had tipped out his last coins at the booking office. She reached into her handbag, took out a small purse and handed it to him.

There were just three foresters sitting in the bar-room. And a black hunting dog. The landlord squatted at their table. They seemed to have been drinking together; now they were all staring at her. 'Bloody hell,' one of them said under his breath.

Four sausages and bread. They sat at a corner table covered in oil-cloth. Above their heads a full-antlered rutting stag on the banks of a blue river.

The foresters raised their voices: '. . . he was belting along with his gob right near the ground when all of a sudden he stops dead in his tracks and his hair's all standing up on end, and I couldn't get him to move an inch . . .'

She knew for certain that she had heard the very same thing before, in this exact pub – amazingly, here too everything repeated itself, those three foresters and the black dog. She knew that the dog had come across the tracks of a raging wild boar. When had she heard it, though? It must have been a long time ago. Yes, she remembered now, it was when her father was still alive, so it must have been during the war or the first year after it. They were walking along a track, though she couldn't recall a thing about it. Then in the evening they reached this pub and three foresters were sitting just by the door with a dog and telling the story of the tusker.

It's very odd, she thought, that they should still be sitting here, that they haven't grown tired of the story yet. On the other hand, don't we all go on listening to the same handful of stories, over and over again?

The landlord placed plates in front of them.

They ate in silence. Suddenly he said, 'Something sad happened to you, didn't it?'

'Yes,' she said. 'I met you,' and she burst out laughing.

'And what about him?'

'Who?'

'You know who.'

'Ah . . .' She had completely forgotten him until that moment. As almost always happened when she wasn't actually with him. No one had ever been so close to her that she would want to think about them all the time.

'Do you love him?'

She shrugged.

'But you must know!'

'Stop that sort of talk! At least over dinner.'

One of the foresters came over to them with three small glasses. He was still young: a ruddy face and cunning eyes. 'How about a toast? To the beauty of this young lady!' He was unable to take his eyes off the bronze coin on the chain around her neck.

He had come over that time too, she recalled. And forced me to drink. Then everyone had laughed. I expect I made a face.

I was five at the time, she realized in alarm. Why had he done it? But she was sure she knew why he came.

'So get it down you,' the forester said irritably, 'or else I'll shoot you in the night. You and that boy. Through the door.'

Laughter came from the other table.

She knew he had come precisely for that laughter, and also so he could get a look at her and have a better idea of everything that was going to happen when he would no longer be able to see.

She stood and took the glass and parting her lips slightly, drained its contents. She detested those final moments: a key on a heavy metal ring; leaving the bar with strangers' eyes on her back. 'Thank you,' she said and smiled at the forester. 'Maybe I'll pay you back some time.'

Then she sat down again. So long as the bed doesn't creak and the landlord doesn't make any comments, and the boy doesn't talk needlessly and it's a bit nice at least. He came back from the counter and handed back her purse.

She opened it absentmindedly, and sorted through the change. Suddenly she realized: 'Wasn't there enough left for a room?' It sounded almost triumphal.

'I don't know . . . I . . . I didn't ask . . .' Then she saw him blush and at that moment she too felt a pang of shame and pushed back her chair noisily.

They walked down the long street of darkened houses with dogs barking from the gardens as they passed. But there was a pure and comforting silence. God I've not done this before, it's really crazy. Then there remained a path through the fields, the scent of acacia, and the only light came from the moon high above: unfamiliar and mysterious.

'Where are we going?' she asked. She stared at the rounded toes of her shoes and tried to make out how badly damaged they were. 'Nowhere, I expect,' she answered herself, 'that's the whole point . . .'

He probably didn't notice the irony. 'Once when I was a boy I ran away from home,' he began. 'With a friend of mine. I didn't know where I was going then either. We took sleeping bags and loads of tinned food . . .'

'Yeah, yeah,' she interrupted him impatiently. 'You slept in the woods and the owls hooted but you weren't scared. Then they caught you at the railway station at Český Krumlov. You didn't even get a beating when you got home and so you fell in love. You were thirteen. She was a geography teacher. She dashed your hopes when you came upon her in the arms of the married PE teacher. So you wrote your first poem. Oh, God! If only you'd written a song, at least!'

'What?' he said, mystified.

'A song,' she repeated. 'But no. All any of you wrote was poems.'

Perhaps she shouldn't have said 'any of you'; he would find that the most hurtful thing. Now he said no more and their journey was even more aimless. And the silence was oppressive.

At length he spoke up once more. 'Why are you always like that? You never want to hear anything!' And when she did not reply he asked her again, 'What do you actually do?'

'Stop it! Stop interrogating me!' Then she said, 'Film. In the archives if you must know.'

'That must be interesting.'

'Awfully!'

Before that she had worked in an accounts department and had never dreamed of anything like it: four films a day; Marlon Brando, Laurence Harvey, Alain Delon; all those kisses, those rendezvous on street corners, those ball gowns, those dinners, those bars and orchestras. The stars: Cybulski, Marilyn Monroe, May Britt. Unfinished stripteases and suggested rapes. War: all that horror and lucky encounters. Successful careers. Railwaymen, turners and miners looking for new relationships. Hooligans. Murder in a bathroom and murder on a deserted road. Many abandoned journeys. Twilight and dawn on deserted trails. Parks. Park benches. Children and pensioners and lovers in parks. Hide-and-seek in parks. Departing trains. Street lights at night. The world through a wet windowpane. The poetry of solitude. The poetry of rain. The poetry of great plains. The poetry of mountains. The poetry of discord. The poetry of war ruins. The poetry of sun between branches. The poetry of the first kiss that ends the film – or starts it. Everything. She knew everything.

The power of the sentence left unsaid. Of the gesture not made. The effectiveness of the hint. The provocativeness of undressing viewed from the rear and of brassieres discarded.

Legs naked up to the thigh. Necks exposed. Down as far as the breasts. The provocativeness of concealed nakedness. Nakedness concealed by a blanket. Nakedness concealed by darkness. Concealed by a table. Nakedness behind a screen. Nakedness wrapped round by a towel. In an untied dressing gown.

She knew everything. She knew precisely why it was worth living. She knew precisely why it was not worth living.

'I'm studying worms,' he said, 'and suchlike stupidities. I'm being examined on them tomorrow.'

They slowly climbed a long shallow incline. They didn't stop until they reached the summit where there stood a low ramshackle chapel. A rugged limestone cliff fell away sharply below. In the valley was a river from which dark paths rose upward. The horizon was far away, several ranges of hills in the night.

'Look!' he pointed.

She was tired and her feet were hot and sore. I ought to take off my shoes, it occurred to her. Whatever possessed me to come here in my stilettos? Whatever possessed me to come at all, in order to stand here in the middle of the night on some unknown rock – she'd never believe it if someone else told her about it. 'So what now?' she said. 'We can hardly stand here gawping for ever!' He turned and gingerly grasped the church door's rusty handle. A warm air drifted from within the chapel, full of the scent of flowers long wilted and burnt wax.

The corpse-like face of the Madonna stared at them from the altar and on the floor lay a threadbare rug.

'What are we going to do here?'

'Nothing,' he said, 'unless you fancy praying.'

She sat down wearily on the rug and leaned back against the low step beneath the altar. She drew her knees up beneath her chin and closed her eyes.

'There's a strange silence here,' she whispered.

'Well that suits you, doesn't it?'

'Yes.' But the silence here was more ponderous than outside. This was a place of vast desolation.

'Do you know how to pray?' she whispered.

'No.'

She didn't know how to pray either. Back in the war her grandmother had taught her the Our Father and the Hail Mary and she herself had mumbled the words she'd learnt the moment the sirens started to wail and the flak to explode, but she had never prayed. She had been only three years old at the time and since then nobody had required her to pray, not even when she was ill or her parents' marriage collapsed and her Dad left home. She had not asked for mercy or help or even revenge, nor had she asked for a blessing on her new father – by that time she was a big girl of ten. She had never prayed or asked for anything. Now it struck her that it must be an odd and marvellous feeling to have someone. Not to have someone to pray to as much as someone to turn to and confide in. It was a long time since she had had someone like that.

And what for anyway, she said to herself bitterly. It's easy to fool yourself. Whether you believe in God or some guy or whatever, you always fool yourself in the end.

'Say something!' she said out loud. 'Don't just sit there like a mummy!'

'I don't feel like it!' he snapped.

She felt the waxen face of the statue behind her, and the

scent of the old flowers aroused her. He was standing some-where behind her, or maybe beside her. All she could see was a bare wall and a tiny window that a strange dim light shone through. But she could hear his breathing. It irritated her. 'Can you sing?'

'A little.'

'Sing something!'

'I don't know anything suitable.'

'That doesn't matter.'

'I can hardly belt out hit songs here, can I?'

'It makes no difference.'

'You're crazy,' he said.

'Well stop breathing, then!'

'What?'

'Go away!' she yelled. 'Or stop breathing!'

'Okay,' he replied.

And now she really couldn't hear anything. As if he had sud-denly disappeared or died and she was left alone here in this deserted spot, totally alone. She knew she lacked the strength to stand up and go out into the darkness, and even if she did stand up, and even if she did find the path, she would have nowhere to go.

She felt a pang of anxiety. Come back and don't be dead, she silently told him. Don't die! Don't go away! Don't struggle! Stay with me! Take me away from here!

'Sing something,' she said quietly.

'Okay.'

She still could not see him, but on the adjacent wall she could now make out his silhouette as he opened his mouth.

He sang very quietly. His voice was pleasant and the melody very simple: slightly soothing and slightly amusing. Soon she stopped being aware of it, even of the words, leaving only random pictures without any meaning: elephants with flags, damp roofs plaited out of football shirts, flocks of flying bears, palm birds, mouse-driven clocks; warm colours, pictures like flickering ink blots. She could still see the moving silhouette, but it was no longer leaning against the wall nearby but standing beneath a tall, white staircase: it belonged to her. She could stretch out her hand and say, Come to me, don't go away, don't struggle, stay with me – she could say it and knew he would understand it and stay with her.

So she said, Come with me! And they were running up an enormous staircase, with thousands of actors milling about, some waving flags, others just mournfully reciting, but they ignored them completely and climbed up and up.

'Not so fast!' they shouted after them. 'The abyss looms before you! Don't lose your heads, youngsters!'

'Take no notice of any of them,' she heard his voice. 'Those old clowns, those fogies, those windbags, those car-driving TV heroes paid to recite anything at all.'

'Let them witter away here,' she said. 'They're quite amusing when they perform here.'

'What can you see?' he asked.

'Everything,' she said. 'It's a total blank but in it I can see everything I ever wanted to see.'

He had stopped singing. For a moment she was alarmed, but the silence was now cheerful and friendly and she was still standing on a thin strip of concrete beyond which lay everything and she could make out his dark silhouette in front of her. Don't let him move, she wished, let everything stay the way it is, we'll stay here together always. Let the morning never come, let this moment last for ever.

She was overcome with a drunken longing for laughter and held her breath; then she felt tears on her cheeks. I'm happy, she realized with amazement.

3

It was a silly song that they had made up during evenings at the student residence when they were feeling totally drained. It had thirty verses. I'll sing her two of them, at most, just to show her how she wide of the mark she was about those poems and then I'll kiss her. But he went on singing more and more verses, staring at her face: motionless and very beautiful. She was beautiful. He could lean down and kiss her, but at the same time she was too remote and indifferent, so he didn't.

It's because I know nothing about her, it struck him, and he didn't take his eyes off her: he was accustomed to staring with concentration for hours on end, imprinting on his memory the shapes of beetles and plants, although he had never taken the trouble to memorize the appearance of a particular person – that tends to be obvious at first sight.

He had watched her from the first moment they were together. At the same time he had registered the journey, the houses, the night, the barking dogs and passing trains. He had also talked a great deal and thought about what he was doing and what he was going to do. But at this very moment he was not thinking about or even noticing anything else, just her and her stillness, and then beneath that stillness he saw with astonishment a slight tremor of hair and eyelashes and at last he saw tears well up and start to fall. And he felt compassion and sympathy; she must be experiencing something terribly painful.

But he would do everything to make her happy! He touched her on the shoulder.

'No!' she blurted out. 'Not here! Not now!'

'Say something! Tell me something about yourself.'

'Yes.'

'You will?'

'Yes,' she said quietly, 'but not now.'

He took her by the hand and they left the chapel. To the north-east the night was gradually receding.

They blundered down the stony path in silence. He helped her and waited. She was extremely tired. Her hair was mussed and there were shadows under her eyes. It would soon be morning and they had not even kissed yet. Just because she had to stay so stupidly silent all the time! Why? What was she waiting for? What was she still waiting for?

He turned to her. 'I'm looking forward to hearing everything.'

She felt his impatience.

'Shall we sit down here?'

'Wait a bit.'

She was very tired and gripped by a peculiar feeling of regret. As if someone had woken her up abruptly from a vivid dream full of colour and powerful emotion. She could neither rouse herself nor go back.

The first cottages of some village emerged out of the darkness. Cocks were crowing like mad, the path grew lighter and the dust was slightly damp.

'Well?' he said.

'Just wait a bit.' Then she asked, 'How will we get home?'

'Do you have to go to work?'

She nodded.

'There'll be some long-distance drivers along soon,' he said. 'They're bound to stop for you.'

But they were walking along a byroad and he knew that no long-distance drivers came this way. He was quite glad they didn't. They had so little time left.

'Come on, let's sit down here!'

She shook her head. What shall I tell him? she thought wearily to herself. That time back then, when the first one took her by the hand . . . It was strange, it had been the very same gesture as his yesterday evening. It hadn't been on a bench but in the empty natural-history study. She recalled the tall green cupboard full of stuffed birds, the toad in alcohol, the tarantulas, the very same gesture as his yesterday. It was strange how many important and involved experiences she had had since – rendezvous and car journeys, protestations, entreaties, threats, men's tears, nights in parks and nights in strange flats, disappointments, hotel beds and separations – but this was something she recalled more clearly than all the rest, and she remembered that touch, how he had covered her hand with his, that lovely touch that was so tender and so long ago.

I'm awfully sentimental, she thought. It must be the lack of sleep.

She closed her eyes slightly and managed to clear her thoughts. Her entire life had collapsed. The feeling of that dream came back to her. She could see the dark outline of a forest below a sky that was turning blue – the charred wall of the city. She could see the faint reflections of the fire: now she was part of a column of marching soldiers that was once more approaching its destination.

Where are you leading me?

I'm leading you soldiers to the future. To a greater love. To a new and more valuable happiness!

No, she said, I don't believe any more. I know I won't be convinced. I'll stay here.

In that case, said the one in front, you'll be a little lost soldier. Little lost soldiers are worst off of all. They're the ones that stumble around an empty field telling themselves they'll conquer something on their own. You'll suffer rain and loneliness and silence, you'll get out of the habit of our regulations and excellent orders, and when the enemy finds you you'll just gibber with fright and he'll slaughter you and there'll be no one there to close your eyes.

I'll stay here with him, she said happily. I'm fond of him.

He suddenly stopped to listen. He was unable to conceal his annoyance. 'Something's coming!'

It was a heavy Tatra truck, with its load covered by a tarpaulin. The driver opened his swollen eyelids wide: 'You've been out gallivanting late,' he said. 'I've never seen the like – four o'clock in the morning!'

He remained silent for a moment, looking first at her, then at him, then back at her.

'Okay, climb aboard,' he said eventually. 'You'll find a bit of space somewhere among the barrels.'

He jumped on board. He could make out the brown oval barrels in the darkness. There was a smell of beer.

She had to take off her shoes and hand them to him. Then she tried to swing her leg over the high tail gate, but her skirt was too tight. He leaned over, gripped her under the armpits and hauled her up. For a moment he held her in his arms with her mouth very close to his.

A bundle of damp, grubby sacks lay by the side board. It was extremely cramped. They sat on the blankets, their elbows touching and their knees drawn up under their chins.

'There you are, then,' he said. 'There you are.'

His face was right next to hers. She could see each of his features in the light that streamed through a hole in the tarpaulin. A boyish face. Quite smooth and unblemished.

He wants me to say I'm fond of him. And he wants to kiss me. I have to find some way of telling him I like him and for that reason don't want to kiss him. Not now. Not now, at least. She knew she had to say something quickly so that he understood her. It was a matter of finding the words, ordinary words: I like you!

So you love me, he will say. Let's go somewhere together, then. No! Some other way. She strained every muscle to find the words and they started to come to her, from a long way away: two lights on a deserted dawn road, a broad sheet of canvas, a quiet whisper from beneath the tarpaulin. It's been an unforgettable evening. Even if we are to share nothing else together, it will have been worth getting to know one another. But we'll never leave each other now!

'You promised me . . .' he said.

'Just stop that!' she snapped at him. How she hated all those clichés. They confined her. They merged with her. They were inside her. She was drenched in them. They were all she could come up with. She couldn't manage anything else. All she could do was kiss him!

So you love me? Let's go somewhere together, shall we?

Where?

To your place maybe.

She tried to stop the film but it was already running.

A little bedroom as dawn is breaking. An unmade bed. I'm afraid it's a bit of a mess.

79

Boyish eyes open wide. It's really nice here! Nervous shuffling. Where should I go while . . .

Turn your back!

A languid feline gesture. Arms raised. A bronze chain being undone.

Outside the window the city awakes. Dustmen. Milk cans.

Detail of a chair. The remaining items of underwear fall.

'There you are then,' he broke the silence. 'We'll be in Prague in a minute. A fat lot you're going to tell me.'

By now he didn't even want to hear anything. He just needed something to take his frustration out on. Frustration at the fact she'd constantly managed to evade him, that he had fallen for that mystique of hers. She had come with him so that he could fill her emptiness for one evening. But he wasn't completely sure. If she were to look at him now, if she were to smile a little bit, he'd take it all back. But no, she remained silent, and he repeated to himself over and over again. An empty, ordinary, empty girl . . . 'So you're not going to tell me anything?' he asked once more.

She tried desperately to find a single sentence, but a meaningless jumble of phrases and protestations swirled around in her head: the tenderest of banalities, the names of animals and flowers, jabbering words – my love, my precious, my darling, my valentine, my copperhead, my sweet boy, my one and only – long lingering glances seemed to pour out of the beer barrels along with the soft sound of kisses. There was nothing else. Nothing at all. She opened her mouth slightly, gulped and shook her head from side to side.

'You . . . you!'

'No,' she said hastily, 'please don't!'

She shook her head stupidly. He clasped her face in his hands, for a short moment her eyes were very close and he was

80

appalled at how motionless they were. 'No,' she said very quietly, 'please don't!'

Then they knelt there on the damp, grubby sacks and kissed.

He kissed her – my love, my precious, my darling, my Snow White, my beautiful, my fragrant, my Lingula, until at last the lorry started to jolt over the cobbles of the city and she whispered, 'Stop it now! Stop it!' And again they sat side by side with their knees under their chins, and his arm around her shoulders. With the stench of beer.

Through the hole in the tarpaulin she could see sooty fragments of walls and roofs and chimneys and her head was clear and she was utterly calm as always when she returned late from a night out.

'Lingula,' he said, 'are you happy?'

Oh, God, back to work again. I'll hardly have time to change and I'll have bags under my eyes. 'You know I am,' she said with a voice that was clear and level.

The lorry pulled up in front of the Electricity Board. She jumped down first. He held her in his arms once more. Then they waited in front of the white-tiled building as a golden mist rose up from the river.

'Shall we go?'

One of the old-style trams came rattling over the bridge. 'I'll take this one,' she said. 'Perhaps you'll let me go now.'

He nodded. 'And when will we see each other again?'

'What for?' she repeated.

She saw the amazement on his face and remorse began to well up in her too. She should have run across the street long ago. But she wanted to say at least something to him.

They faced each other in silence. 'What's "Lingula"?' she remembered.

At last he could get his own back for all her silence.

'Lingula? Stop that! Your tram's about to leave!'

He watched her run across the wide, deserted road junction.

He couldn't understand how she could leave just like that. Without a single word. Had it all really meant nothing to her? Could she really have felt nothing of what he had felt? For a moment pain gripped his mouth and throat and he was obliged to swallow several times to ease it slightly. He saw her leap into the open tram car as it started to pull away. It was time for him to go too but he waited. She was still standing on the steps of the tram. She could have turned her head at least.

She stood on the dirty steps. She was getting back very late again but it didn't matter. It had been a remarkable night – a pity it couldn't have lasted, a pity the lorry had turned up, a pity the morning had come, a pity he was like all the others . . .

Someone behind her shouted, 'Climb aboard, miss!'

She moved to the top step and the tram screeched its way round the bend. Maybe he's still standing there. She wanted to lean out and check, but she was being jostled into the car. She caught sight of an empty seat. At last she realized just how tired she was. The conductor clipped her ticket – the dark-coloured tram uniform – he smiled slightly, possibly at her, but more likely at the bronze coin – it felt out of place at this time of the morning.

She half closed her eyes and could suddenly see the dark silhouette and it occurred to her that even if she were to shut her eyes tight or run away from it as far as she could, she would still see it – motionless on the dark wall nearby. It was inside her. She could reach out and touch it, saying, Come with me, don't leave, don't struggle, stay by me, and he would be with her at last and never leave her. She took her ticket and smiled back.

The time on the large street clock was 5.30 a.m. He had to be in for his exam by eight-thirty. Nobody else will have prepared themselves in such a sensational fashion. An entire afternoon, evening and night. With her. And in the end she kissed me. They're not going to believe that.

Lingula, he said to her in his mind, *lingula*, he recited silently, a genus of the order of brachiopods, the shells either open or closed in the anterior free part of the shell that has embedded bristles. Like this entire group of worms, the *lingula* is closely related to the order of phoronids . . .

(1962)

HEAVEN, HELL, PARADISE

He thought it best to park two blocks from her building. When he got out he looked around carefully, but there was too much traffic to work out whether there had been a car tailing him.

He entered the building and stood waiting, hidden behind the front door. He noticed the thumping of his heart but what worried him more than the thought of being followed was how he would be received, half a year on, by the woman he had returned for. He had no idea, the last time they parted, that it would be for so long. And it could have been for ever if he'd made the same decision as most people in his situation. He should have phoned her beforehand, except that phones couldn't be trusted. He took a quick look into the street but there was no sign of anyone suspicious.

So he went up to the first floor, noticing the familiar odour of turpentine and thinner that escaped into the passage from inside the flat. There was the same painted plaque on the door:

a couple lying on a bed with *Jan and Milada Kaska* inscribed in copperplate. He rang the bell.

For a moment there was no sound. She couldn't be home, although – at least in the days when he'd had an interest in her timetable – she didn't usually leave the house until the afternoon. Then came the sound of familiar footsteps and the rattle of the lock. She was wearing make-up and an unfamiliar outfit, apparently on her way out somewhere.

'You're here?' To his surprise, she blushed. 'You're crazy, Doc! What if he was home?'

'He's got a job to go to.' He stepped inside and kissed her.

'You're crazy, you're crazy,' she repeated. 'What are you doing here? You were abroad!'

'Yes, but you were here.'

'These days everyone's going in the opposite direction. Haven't you heard?'

'I couldn't care less what other people do.'

'You're crazy. They'll put you in jail, sooner or later. And if they don't they'll sort you out, so you won't know where you are.'

'I'll be with you. There's no point in trying to get me to change my mind now I'm here. Can you spare a moment?'

'I had no idea you were coming. There's no way I could have known.'

He tried to put his arms round her, but she broke free of him. 'What do you think you're doing? How do you know I want you?'

'I can come some other time. I'll be able to now.'

'I would have thought that depended on me too – whether I feel like having you.'

'I came because of you. I came because I wanted you so much I couldn't bear it any longer.'

'What nonsense are you talking?' She finally retreated from the front hall into the living room and he followed her. The room was the same as when he was last there, apart from some new paintings on the walls which must have been her own work. She didn't sit down or offer him a seat. 'So you've come back for me?' she said with a shrug. 'It's your business why you've returned – I hope you don't think it's mine?' She was standing opposite him and staring at him as if he were a total stranger. As if she had forgotten all the days and nights they had spent together, when they'd exchanged endless protestations of love. 'I wasn't expecting you. You're crazy. You take me by surprise like this and immediately fling yourself at me. I'd already forgotten about you. After all there was no point waiting for you once I realized I'd never see you again.'

'I thought about you all the time!'

'It's your business if you thought about me.' She started. Someone was stamping up the stairs. A dog barked on the other side of the wall.

She came up close to him. 'You can't stay here!'

'Is he due back about now?'

'You act as though he was the only person in the world. It so happens he's gone off. He's far away. All he left me were these,' and she showed him two slim booklets. The green one was a savings book, the red one was clearly an identity card. 'Everyone's going off somewhere. I'm the only one hanging around.'

'Did he go in the same direction?'

'He went off on a business trip and it makes no difference what direction he went in. But a couple of dozen relatives have keys to this flat.'

'We'll take a trip somewhere. I've got my car here!'

'You're crazy, a complete nutcase. You've been away for about a hundred years and you turn up here expecting me to be ready and waiting with my nightdress and change of shoes in a suitcase . . .'

'Yes,' he said, 'that's exactly what I expected. When's he getting back?'

'I've no idea. I didn't ask. And anyway, people can return unexpectedly – didn't you know?'

'I suppose so, if they're deeply in love,' he conceded.

'Or off their head. Just hang on for a moment. I have to make a phone call.'

The hotel had recently been renovated. The room was on the fifth floor at the very end of a corridor and was doing its best to look modern. The walls had been covered in blue wallpaper and the divans had been given colourful cretonne covers. The same material had been used to cover the armchairs and even the fixed-station radio receiver. On the glass-covered table top lay a bottle opener. However, instead of a bottle there was a telephone and a folder of writing paper.

'Can you see that neon sign?' she asked.

Immediately above their window shone a red and white fluorescent tube. The light from it came through the window onto their beds. 'We've a room with neon,' she laughed.

He put his arms round her. She let him kiss her and then pushed him away. 'Wait. I'm all sticky from that car ride.' She went into the bathroom, but as in the old days she left the door half open. Everything was like the old days, just as it ought to be. Up to this moment he still hadn't been sure it was wise to have returned, but now he knew he had made the right decision. His place was here. His place was wherever he knew she was close by.

The window opened onto the square. In the centre was a church and a small park. Opposite was the bus station, without a single bus parked there. Instead two foreign military vehicles stood waiting. He wasn't used to them yet. He wiped the sweat from his forehead. 'It's hot here,' he said. 'Don't you think it's hot in here?'

She didn't reply; maybe she hadn't heard him. There were a few pensioners sitting in the little park as well as some man who happened to be staring into the hotel windows at that moment.

On his way back the frontier crossing had been conspicuously deserted, although it was only seven in the evening. 'Doctor Sláma,' a man in uniform read in his passport. 'Sláma.' The fellow checked through some list for a moment, while he himself looked to see where a Soviet soldier might be hiding or an enemy machine gun poking out. But neither of them found anything suspicious. Amazingly enough he wasn't on the list. Or more likely they hadn't received the proper list yet. The frontier guard returned his passport. 'Drive on.' It was quite easy to get in. But that was true about all traps. He had no doubt he was entering a trap, he even realized that he had set the bait himself. But he belonged here. He belonged where she was.

He wiped his forehead again.

'That guy at reception,' she said, behind him. 'I didn't like the way he looked at us.' She had already taken off her clothes and was wearing only a short nightdress and a lot of make-up. If her face had been as perfect as her figure she wouldn't have to use make-up at all. He gazed at her. He gazed at the woman for whom he had walked into the trap.

'He wasn't sitting there so you could like the way he looked at you.'

'I didn't like the way he looked at *you*.'

'Maybe he just envied me.'

'Maybe,' she conceded, 'but you know the way things are these days. I wouldn't want anybody particularly noticing that I've been here. That I've been here with you. Did you shout something at me when I was in the bathroom?'

'No. I just said how hot it is in here.'

'I'm glad. I like the heat. If I'd had my way I would have been born somewhere in Africa.'

'You were born in just the right place. Just where I had a chance of meeting you.' He hugged her and this time she let him lead her to the couch.

'Or in Brazil,' she added. 'It's hot in Brazil too. And they dance there as well. That's where they have that famous carnival, isn't it? Or isn't it?'

He undressed quickly.

'I know you're not interested in carnivals. It's not the sort of sophisticated entertainment you go in for. What if I were to find us some music?' she suggested and reached out for the radio.

There was a man's voice speaking in ingratiating tones, They have remained quite openly where basically they always were: on the side of counter-revolution.

'I don't want that!' she said interrupting the voice. 'They go on like that all the time now. Do you know that you've already been mentioned? I heard it one day by chance. I put on music when I'm drawing, and they mix that sort of rubbish in with the music. Just in little drops. And before you can reach the knob to switch it off they're playing music again.'

He would have liked to ask her what they had said about

him, but he realized there would be no point asking. She had registered his name, but the rest of the message had escaped her. Her concerns were her drawing, love and perhaps travel still. At most she was willing to listen to interesting stories. As long as they had nothing to do with politics, illness or anything serious.

He lay down by her.

'I'm at your side again, darling. Every night of those six months I imagined this moment.'

'You imagined me? It lasted you a good while, just imagining me.'

'But now I'm here.'

'Yes. Now you're here. And you're shivering all over. You're shivering despite the heat in here.'

'It's you making me shiver.'

'I've given you a fever! Shiver more! More! Even more!' She breathed quickly. She closed her eyes, while he continued to look at her. He knew every feature of her face. The artificial shadows under her eyes. The bluish green make-up on her eyelids. Then he too closed his eyes. Now all he could hear was her moaning. 'You're my love.'

'Ah. How much do you love me?'

'More than my life. More than anything. More than everything. That's why I came. Really.'

'Why do you love me so much?'

'I don't know. I really don't know.'

'Really, really,' she repeated. 'Did we really make love just now?'

'Yes. For the first time in ages I knew I really existed. Over there it was just a bad dream. I used to walk along the street and see you everywhere in those foreign towns where you couldn't be. I saw you in every woman with long hair.'

'In every woman with long hair? Did it matter whether she was dark or blonde?'

'She had to have hair like yours.'

'She had to have black hair, short legs and a threadbare skirt. And did you make love to them when you saw me in them?'

'You know I didn't. Every day without you was pointless. I couldn't bear it any longer.'

'You bore it for quite a while,' she said, 'and I'm glad you bore it.'

'What do you mean?'

'I can't stand the feeling that someone can't bear to be without me, that I have to be with him just because he can't stand to be without me.'

'You're with me because you like being with me.'

'Yes, that's the only reason I was with you. What's the time?'

'I don't know. My watch stopped at the border. It couldn't handle the stress.'

'The watch didn't want to go with you. It had more sense than you had.'

'It had no one to come back to,' he said. 'Should I phone for the time?'

'No. It makes no difference what time it is, anyway.'

'We've only been here a little while,' he said. 'I'm hardly twelve hours back. In this country. Back home.'

'You don't feel at home yet?'

'I used to dream about it almost every night. I used to dream about you. I would be calling you from a phone booth but I'd never manage to dial the right number. Or I'd be waiting for you somewhere round the corner from your street, but you never came.'

'I expect I was somewhere with Jan. I have to be with him sometimes, since he's my husband,' she said. 'You realize I'm married, don't you?'

'But now you're with me,' he said as he embraced her.

'Do you want to do that again already?'

'We've so much lost time to make up for.'

She laughed. 'And then what will we do?'

He remembered he hadn't eaten a thing since morning. 'Then we'll go downstairs,' he suggested. 'There's a restaurant. A little one. It used to be good. Ten years ago.'

'Did you come here then?'

'Yes.'

'With some girl?'

'Yes, at that time you were . . . you were barely fifteen.'

'And you were twenty-six. Did you make love that time?'

'It's not important. I didn't know you in those days.'

'True,' she admitted. 'But you shouldn't repeat things.'

'Do you mean making love?'

'I mean everything.'

'We won't order the same dish.'

'No, we'll have tomato soup. You didn't have tomato soup that time?'

'I don't think so.' He tried to recall the name of that girl. He wanted to say that he couldn't remember the name of the girl he was with, let alone what they had had to eat, but he was afraid she would feel humiliated, seeing it as a premonition of how he would forget her one day, and at that moment he suddenly remembered they had eaten toast with a very hot sauce and the girl's name was Dora. They had also drunk red wine and eaten liver with pineapple and he had spent almost all his month's money, but that was how he lived in those days. They had both got drunk and then gone back to the hotel room, which didn't have blue wallpaper yet, of course, and where the beds were old and creaked. They had made love to the accompaniment of springs creaking and laughed about it.

'And then something absolutely ordinary,' she said, 'like dumplings fried with egg and a cucumber salad. Do you think they'll have a cucumber salad? And then we'll go to the cinema.'

'I'll let you have whatever you want, my love.'

She curled around him and he had the blissful feeling he always had when she touched him. She excited him even when he was dog tired, even when they had made love many times already. 'Darling.'

'What's the time?' she asked afterwards. 'Whatever can the time be?'

'I don't know. I never know when I'm with you. But there is one thing I do know.'

'And what's that?'

'That it's lovely to be with you. I don't want to leave this room. I hate the thought of your having to get dressed.'

'Aha,' she said. 'We're going to stay in this bedroom for ever. And we'll just go on doing those things. But you promised me dinner.'

'That's true.' He sat up. If he craned his neck a bit he could see right down into the square. Pedestrians were hurrying past the park. It was only just evening. He turned back to her once more. 'It's so long since I've seen you. It's so long since I've been with you.'

'That light above your head,' she said. 'You look like a saint or an icon. But I expect saints weren't suppose to do things like this all the time.' She reached out for him. 'Why are you getting up then?' Her hand stroked his thigh lightly. 'When did you get back?'

'Today, of course.'

'You must be tired. We don't have to go anywhere. I'll lose a bit of weight at least. I put on weight when you were away. I missed the exercise!' She laughed. 'Tell me what sort of time you had there.'

'I've told you. I couldn't bear to be without you.'

'Did you have a girlfriend?'

'Yes, but I wasn't in love with her. I can't love anyone else the way I love you.'

'What was she like? Have you got a photo of her with you?'

'No!'

'Didn't she give you a photo when she heard you were coming here to me?'

'There's something I'm beginning to remember . . .' The scene returned to him so powerfully that he could actually see the cripple and if he'd been able to draw like her, he could have sketched a portrait of him. 'I found myself a really miserable job at Waterloo – nothing to do with medicine. I used to travel to it every morning. One day when I was getting on the underground train in Finchley there was a little guy on crutches standing there staring by the newspaper stand. He wasn't buying or selling anything, just leaning on his crutches gaping. He was still young and he was ginger-haired the way that only the English can be, or rather the Welsh or the Scots. And he was staring at me. He had to go and choose me out of all people. He was smiling but it wasn't a pleasant smile, there was something cunning or hateful about it.'

'And were you scared of him?'

'No. I somehow knew I needn't be afraid of him.'

'Is that all?' she asked when he fell silent.

'No. That was only the beginning.'

She pressed him to her. 'Do you still love me?'

'Yes. I love you so much that I had to come back and didn't care what would happen to me.'

'Do you think they'll put you in prison?'

'It doesn't matter. I knew I couldn't stay somewhere I had no chance of seeing you.'

'I wouldn't want them to send you to prison. At least not now that I'm with you,' she explained. 'That guy at reception – didn't you notice the way he was looking at you?'

He shook his head. 'I wasn't looking at him. My eyes were on you.'

'You ought to have been looking. You ought to be a little wary – when you're with me, at least. I'm married, don't forget. But you didn't finish telling me about the ginger man.'

'Oh, yes. Well, just imagine, when I got off the underground at Waterloo station that fellow was standing at the top of the escalator. He was standing there watching me as I rose towards him.'

'I expect he was tailing you. And he'd come there by car.'

'At that time of day the underground is the fastest way to go. He was standing there on his crutches. Ginger and smirking. No, he didn't follow me. He went off towards the exit and didn't look back once. So I decided to follow him, even though I was on my way to work. He was making for some working-class houses that are all over that area, and I set off after him. He lurched along on those crutches like a walking scarecrow. Eventually he disappeared inside one of the houses – a working-class brick house. I hesitated for a moment but I knew I had to go in after him. The passage was lined with doors and no other way out. I should have left, but instead I started to ring their bells one by one. It occurred to me that I wouldn't leave, that I couldn't leave, until he had opened his door and explained to me how he came to be at the station. But he didn't open up. I started to thump one of the doors and shout. I made such a racket that it must have been heard on the street, but the door didn't open and the silence inside seemed to me almost deathly. Like the first time I set foot in an autopsy room or a mortuary. I've no idea where the fellow disappeared to. Unless he jumped out of the window. With those crutches.'

He was so absorbed in his story that for a moment he had forgotten all about her. Now he looked in her direction. She was asleep.

He got up. The heat was almost unbearable. He went over to the window and tried in vain to open it. Even the floor tiles in the bathroom were warm. He turned on the cold-water tap but nothing came out. So he ran a little hot water into the basin and washed his face. He caught the sound of footsteps quietly approaching in the corridor. They stopped when they reached their door.

He waited for them to start moving away again, but silence had descended on the corridor again. He realized that he was afraid. He ought to open the door and find out who, if anyone, was standing outside, but he couldn't bring himself to do it. He stood there wet, naked, tense and alert in the middle of a strange bathroom in a country which, although he had decided to come back to it, was in reality now also alien to him, and his fear increased by the moment.

He returned to the bedroom. She was sleeping. Red and white reflections played on her naked body. Why were the windows here sealed? Why had the desk clerk watched him so closely? Did he know him from somewhere?

He continued to listen intently. There was still no sound from the corridor. Outside a car sounded its horn and from a long way off a strange rumble started to approach. It could be the sound of machines in an unseen factory or the sound of tanks on the move. Whose tanks? All tanks were under the same unified enemy command. Why had he returned, in fact? Had he really come back on account of the woman who happened to be with him at this moment but actually belonged to another man? Had he returned for this moment of ecstasy that he could have found more easily elsewhere, as he'd never had a problem finding women to experience it with?

He sat down in the armchair. He took a sheet of writing paper out of the folder and started to fold it into a shape he remembered from his childhood. He no longer felt any yearning, or even happiness at being close to the woman he had yearned for. He felt hungry, tired and vaguely uneasy. Where would he go tomorrow? And the following day? He was too old to go back to his parents and he had no home of his own. All he had was a room for tonight and tomorrow morning. Unless he prolonged the stay and persuaded her to remain a day or two longer. The thought of having to leave the room and go out into the street seemed unbearable.

The rumble of the distant tanks did not stop. He completed the shape and laid it to one side on the glass table top. Then he got ready to start another one.

'Doc,' he heard from behind him, 'what are you up to? Why aren't you here with me?'

He started. 'It's a sort of game.' He inserted his fingers into the paper pockets and opened and closed the paper mouth.

Heaven, hell, paradise
where's your soul to go?
Into heaven, into hell
Just like so.

'Where are you now?' she asked.

He listened to the roaring from outside. He thought it was coming closer. When the soldier knocked down the door, he ought to tackle him. But the only weapon he had available was the bottle opener. 'Here,' he replied, 'with you.'

'And what about your soul?'

'I don't know if I have a soul.' When he was small he had believed he had one and that it was immortal, but he had seen too many people die since then, and little had remained of their souls after their brain cells had been eroded by old age or disease. He was going to say something more but she spoke first. 'No, you don't have a soul. That's why you're able to do those things so well!'

Yes, that's what he was to her – a means of pleasure. While he happened to be around. Who had been the means when he was away?

'What's hell?' she asked.

He shrugged. He knew she wasn't expecting a serious answer. None the less he said, 'I went to see a play when I was over there. There were these people shut in one room, where they were together all the time. For eternity, you understand – the same people. That was the author's idea of hell.'

'And what's yours?'

'I don't know. I think hell is different things for different people. Hell is being defenceless when someone is pointing a pistol at you and telling you he's doing it because he loves you.

Hell is suffering. Having a bad conscience. Being bored. Listening to lies. Hearing the truth. Losing your freedom . . .'

'You're beating about the bush. And how about paradise? Do you know what paradise is, at least?' she asked.

It struck him that paradise was a state of innocence. Being unaware of evil. The absence of fear. He could only think of negative definitions. Paradise was the presence of God, of course, and hence the absence of death. Therefore paradise was a delusion. But there was no sense in saying any of that out loud. So all he said was, 'I would like to be with you entirely one day. And for you to be with me alone.'

'I've been entirely with you today,' she pointed out. 'Do you think I could be with you even more than that?'

'You wouldn't have to leave me for someone else, there would be just the two of us. In a secluded house with a garden.'

'Just a moment ago you were saying that was precisely what that play thought was hell.'

'But it would be possible to leave that house. And have visitors.'

'Yes. And lie out in the garden and sunbathe. In Brazil. Or Spain. Would we have a swimming pool?'

'Why not?'

'Okay. That villa could stand right by the seaside; that would be even better. And in the evenings we'd visit some little tavern or pizzeria. What would we drink?'

'Wine,' he suggested.

'Wine, naturally. But what kind?'

'That would depend on what we were eating. You'd drink the kind of wine that happened to take your fancy.' Then he remembered, 'Do you remember that little hotel by the dam? We were there all on our own and the woman in charge brought us Italian wine wearing a ball gown.'

'No,' she said, shaking her head.

'Ruffino. We drank a whole bottle of it though we weren't able to make love. There wasn't anywhere handy – you had to be home that evening.'

'No,' she said, 'I never remember things that have happened. I expect I had to get home, if you say so. You know I'm married, don't you? But now I'm with you and at this moment I'm ready to drink any old wine. What is the time, anyway?'

'I don't know. It must be fairly late. Perhaps midnight. Can you hear that rumbling? Are those tanks?'

'Is the restaurant closed already?'

'Yes, I expect so. Listen to it, for heaven's sake!'

'You promised me tomato soup!'

'Don't think about it now. It's too late. I haven't eaten today either. Not a thing.'

'But you've got a different stomach, haven't you,' she said. 'It's no consolation to me that you're hungry too. Won't you put on some music, at least?'

He turned the knob. 'They've packed up already. It's late. They've switched it off so that the hotel guests don't disturb each other. Though mind you . . .' Someone's attempt to prevent him being disturbed seemed absurd at that moment. In this country. And to the sound of distant engines and caterpillar tracks.

'I'm thirsty,' she said. 'Bring me some water, at least.'

The tiles were still warm and still only the hot water worked. Once more the sound of creeping feet came from the other side of the door. Hell is fear, it struck him. And paradise is the absence of fear, the certainty of safety. The certainty of loyalty. That was why paradise was a delusion.

She drank several gulps of warm water. 'What are you standing there for? Why don't you come here, at least, seeing you don't want to go anywhere any more? Or don't you love me now?'

'If I didn't love you I wouldn't be here.' And he had a longing, an absurd longing, for certainty, for safety, for her loyalty.

She clung to him. 'And we wanted to go to the cinema,' she said ruefully.

'We will go. We'll go often, you'll see.'

'Do you think so? I don't know that we'll ever go again. But I wanted to go today. Maybe they won't even send you to prison. Maybe you just imagined it all.'

'What did I imagine?'

'The business with that hunchback. You just imagined it. You've got nothing to worry about.'

'He was lame,' he corrected her.

'I'd be more afraid of that guy at reception. He'll tell them you're here if they ask. All of a sudden there'll be a knock on the door and it'll be them. And I'll cop it along with you!'

'They don't know I'm here.'

'They don't know you're here?' she said in amazement. 'But they put you in the register.'

'I didn't show them my identity card. I borrowed your husband's when I was at your place. They never check the photo, they just want the document. I thought it would be better for you if I didn't sign in under my own name.'

'You borrowed his identity card and didn't even tell me? So I'm actually here with my husband. I've simply been fulfilling my conjugal duties.'

'Are you cross?'

'No. Why should I be?' she said in surprise. 'My only worry is that you won't love me so much if you think I'm just fulfilling my conjugal duties.'

'I love you. Nobody could love you more than I do.'

'That's why you came so far,' she said. 'To prove it. And you registered under his name, so it was actually him who's been showing his prowess. I love you for that.'

'I want you to love me for eternity.'

'"Eternity"? Eternity and really. You always use the funniest words. Isn't it enough that I'm here with you?'

When he woke up it was already getting light. There was someone walking up and down the corridor and it filled him with such terror that beads of sweat stood out on his forehead. He listened to the strange footsteps without moving. They went away and then came back again. Someone was standing guard outside the door. His head ached. Most likely due to the heat and the agitation, not to mention the lack of sleep and hunger, possibly.

She lay next to him, asleep. She hadn't washed last night and make-up was smeared over her eyelids and cheeks and there were droplets of sweat on her forehead. A puffy, smudgy, ordinary woman. She was the reason he'd returned. She was the reason he'd walked into a trap.

He was hungry. He quietly opened his suitcase. Several dirty shirts, some magazines and a folded suit. Not a single sweet or even chewing gum. He closed the case again.

'What are you rummaging for?' came her voice. 'You don't happen to have a pistol there, do you? People like you have to carry a weapon, don't they? And don't look at me now. I'm ugly in the morning.' He heard her footsteps and then from the bathroom the sound of running water.

She emerged naked, but immaculately made up once more. 'Do you still find me attractive?'

'You're beautiful. The most beautiful girl I've ever seen. You must believe me that I couldn't bear it there without you any more.'

'I believe you. What are we going to do now?' she asked. 'Do you think they're serving breakfast yet?'

'I doubt it.' And he was startled by the thought that he would soon have to abandon this close, airless room.

'There's no reason why they shouldn't bring it up to us,' she said. 'Call them and tell them we want our breakfast here.'

He lifted the receiver and waited for someone to reply.

'I'll have ham,' she said. 'Ham and eggs and tea. I love tea, I could drink it all day long.'

'It's dead.' There was no point fooling themselves. They were trapped. No trick with a borrowed identity card was going to help him. They were outside the door waiting for him to emerge.

'Don't,' she said. 'We'll go downstairs. What shall I put on?'

'Nothing. I like you best when you've got nothing on.'

'Do you think I ought to have breakfast in the nude? Or are you going to bring me breakfast in bed? Will you go down and fetch it?'

He nodded and stepped over to the window. It was already dawn. There were several buses waiting at the bus station. Below, almost indiscernible from five floors up, a man on crutches hurried about on a narrow strip of grass. A ball flew towards him from some unseen opponent around the corner. The man on crutches hobbled over and kicked the ball. He observed the game, watching the ball fly back and forth – watching his imminent fate.

'What can you see there?' she asked.

'Nothing.' Although he sensed that he was to see him again, he couldn't yet work out how and where it might happen.

'Is that your hunchback?' she said, looking over his shoulder.

He shrugged and stretched out on the bed. The paper game lay on the table. Where's your soul to go?

'He's fallen over,' she called from the window. 'He slipped as he tried to kick the ball. It's only a young lad. That fellow wasn't a young lad, was he?'

'Do you love me?' he asked.

'I don't know. At this moment I'm hungry. How am I supposed to think about whether I love you when I'm thinking about ham and eggs?'

'Come over here. I want you.'

'Let's go and eat instead.'

'Afterwards. They're not open yet anyway.'

'We can buy a roll at a shop.'

'Afterwards.'

'You're crazy. You always want to make love and never want to eat!' She knelt at the side of the bed and placed her lips on his. She let herself be kissed. 'That's why I love you: because you're crazy. And now come on!'

He could feel the apprehension sneaking up on him. Where will I run to? But so long as he was here, so long as he was with her, so long as he could hear her breath and cling to her body, he remained, he was still alive and had one certainty: her. He could touch her, feel her closeness, and that awoke in him a sense of blissfulness and peace. He put his arms around her and drew her to him, kissing her, his lips weary and dry. I love you. Don't leave me! Stay with me!

She made love with him in silence and that made him even more uneasy. 'Just a little while longer,' he whispered, 'and then we'll go.'

When he next awoke the room was bathed in light,

although he was sure he'd slept only a few minutes. She was in the bathroom again. In the corridor footsteps went back and forth. Men's, women's, maybe even children's footsteps. A medley of footsteps. He sat down and looked out of the sealed window.

'Is he there?' she asked from behind him.

'No, he isn't, sweetheart.' He looked at her. She was already half dressed. No, she'll leave. He had no one to hold on to any more.

'Are we going to eat?' she asked. 'They must be open by now. It can't be far off midday. I'll have soup. I'll eat two servings of soup and three rolls. Will they have fresh rolls?'

'Don't get dressed yet, darling!'

'We have to go now. I've got to be home this afternoon. You don't have to drive me if you don't feel like it. I'll thumb a lift.'

'I'll drop you home. I want to. I want to be with you.'

'You're tired and I'm hungry.' She sat down next to him. She kissed him. 'Come on, my pet. We'll leave the things here and come back here for a little afterwards!'

He didn't move. Nor did the time. He stood motionless in the blue hotel room. The blue cell. The sun bobbed out of the mist and its rays heated the hot air even more.

'Have you got something to read here?'

'No, only magazines.'

'Read to me. Read me something.'

'They're specialized journals.'

'That's fine. They'll take your mind off things, at least.'

'They're English.'

'That doesn't matter. You can translate them for me, can't you?'

He got up and opened his case. The suitcase and the things

in it were from over there – where she was absent, but so was fear. Then he leaned over her. Her lips were tightly pursed and her eyes half closed. He looked for a moment at that unfamiliar face. "'From ancient times",' he translated, '"doctors were interested in the construction of the human skeleton. They noticed that bone had different characteristics from all other tissue . . ."'

'What sort of bones do cripples have?' she asked.

'That all depends. Do you really want me to explain it?'

'Yes, really,' she grinned at him. 'Really and at length . . .'

He remained silent. Love was the only thing they ever talked about together. There was no point in reading aloud to her. He closed the journal and tossed it on to the floor.

'Come on. We will be coming back, after all.'

He put his arms around her.

'Leave me alone!' she said crossly.

'Don't you love me any more?'

'You're crazy and I'm hungry.'

Dust swirled in the beam of sunlight. He felt the urge to go and look out the window at the patch of grass. But he resisted it.

'You don't love me either,' she said. 'You're just scared. You've been scared ever since you entered this room. You're scared of every footstep outside the door, you're scared of being left here on your own. You're longing for some certainty. Jesus,' she burst out, 'what are you doing here with me? Why didn't you stay over there and find yourself some nice, faithful woman?' She stood up.

He reached out and tried to draw her to him.

'Don't touch me!' she shouted, scratching at his chest. Her nails gouged out long bloody furrows.

'Darling, don't leave me now!' He watched her dress. The scratches stung. He felt his own blood running down his chest.

He switched on the radio – at last there was some music. He wasn't aware of it, only of his tiredness and the hunger that filled his body with inertia. He was aware of his inertia and uncertainty. What will happen next? I'll close my eyes and stay lying here. I'll have a sleep. Towards evening I'll get up and have something to drink. One has to drink, at least. He was aware of his thirst. He got up and went to the bathroom and drank two glasses of hot water, one after the other.

She sat in front of the mirror combing her hair. 'What sort of hair did she have, the one who was here?'

'Does it make a difference?'

'Did you torture her with hunger, too?'

'No, things were different in those days.'

'Things are always different. Why are you lying down again? You don't mean to stay here, do you?'

He broke into a sweat. He shouldn't have drunk so much water. But it didn't matter. He tried to listen carefully to the sounds from the corridor and from outside, but the music drowned out everything else.

'What *are* you scared of, in fact?' she asked. 'Did you kill someone over there?'

'Maybe people who kill are better off than people who don't.'

'Do you think so?' She was beautiful once more.

Blood trickled from the scratches on his chest. He thought he heard some footsteps, close by. Then someone seized the door handle. He started to panic. 'Could you switch that radio off for a moment?'

His eyes were glued to the door handle. It didn't move.

Maybe they won't come, while she's here. 'Do you love me a bit?'

'At this moment I'm hungry,' she said.

'Will you leave without me?'

She took him by the hand. 'Come on,' she said. 'Come on.'

As if there was any point eating. He listened for footsteps in the corridor. One step, another and then a strange knocking sound. One step, another and then the knock. 'Can you hear?' he asked and held his breath.

'I don't want to stay here any more!' She let go of his hand.

Someone had stopped in front of the door and was quietly sliding a key into the lock.

She turned towards him and a look a horror came on her face.

'Don't be afraid,' he said. 'I'll protect you.'

'You're bleeding,' she noticed. 'How come you're bleeding?'

She leaned towards him and kissed his chest.

He felt her lips suck at his chest, he felt her cool fingertips and he felt his bleeding slow. 'My darling,' he whispered. He knew they were touching each other for the last time. This was the last time he would say those words to her. She was leaving. She didn't need his protection or his love. She didn't need his return or his sacrifice. She was leaving like the rest, like everything. It was impossible to hold on to things, it was impossible to return. Nothing could be returned, that was the only certainty, the chilling, depressing certainty that everything would pass, including this moment and this anxiety. He could calmly close his eyes. And peace really began to envelop him and he was deaf even to the thumping of strangers' fists on the door. He sank into the bed.

They came in. There were two of them. The first was the

desk clerk, now dressed in blue overalls, the second was a young man with bright ginger hair, who walked with a stick. In his left hand he carried a large travelling bag.

'So what's going on?' said the first of the men. 'What's up with you? You should have vacated the room ages ago.'

She stood up and hastily wiped her mouth. With the other hand she pulled up the covers to hide her lover's nakedness. 'We were sleeping, that's all. He's still asleep,' she said and walked quickly past the two men and out of the door, as if she were ashamed that they had found her still there. The desk clerk went over to the bed. 'Wakey, wakey Mr Kaska!' Then he turned to the ginger-haired young man. 'Christ, did you get a look at her?' and he smacked his lips softly.

The ginger-haired man put his walking stick and his bag down on the armchair. Then his eye fell on the folded paper game. 'Heaven, hell, paradise.' He spoke the words tenderly. 'Paradise,' he repeated and he glanced out of the open door, as if in hope of catching another glimpse of her.

(1969)

HONEYMOON

1

The road wound upwards with hairpin bends.

The girl sat pressed to his shoulder. Smaller and more finely built, she was almost hidden by him.

He drove with one hand, his other arm round the girl. Over that year he had become used to driving in that mildly uncomfortable one-handed fashion and the two of them had travelled like that across half of Europe, the German autobahns, the oddly deserted road between Chalons and Meaux lined with maple trees that seemed to have been gnawed by the wind (maybe they weren't even maples; it had been a misty night) and the wild mountain range of Olympus between Kozani and Tyrnavos, and amazingly, the whole time, even after endless hours of driving, he had always been aware of her, the touch of her hand or the trembling of her body, and would kiss her sometimes as they drove along – they would kiss while tearing along countless instantly forgotten roads and make love in that car on deserted country tracks at night, or in the middle of the day, when the sun beat down on her pale, not particularly beautiful face, while a Greek shepherd slowly passed on a lazy donkey. And now again they were approaching one of their destinations that was not really a destination, the roofs of a little town peeking out from behind the tops of coloured trees, looking almost like a stage backdrop in the light of the setting sun.

'So you've gone and got married on me,' he said, and it didn't sound like a rebuke, more like a recollection of her state, simply a sentence intended to break the silence for a moment.

'I've gone and got married on you,' she repeated. 'But I'm on my honeymoon with you,' and she opened wide her fish-like eyes as she always did when she declared something that was beyond doubt. 'This is my honeymoon, because I've just got married, and yours because you're with me!'

'Yes,' he conceded, slightly amazed.

'I couldn't have married *you*, could I?' she said, nudging him with her shoulder. 'Or could I?'

'I don't think so,' he admitted.

'With you I can just go on a honeymoon.'

'We've been on lots of honeymoons,' he said.

'You think we've already been on lots of honeymoons, then?' she asked.

'It doesn't matter though,' he added quickly. 'This is the first time you've actually been married. This time it's a real honeymoon,' he said, playing along, and then braked, turning the wheel with his free hand, and drove past a baroque fountain before pulling up in front of a house that might once have been gothic.

'It's not a particularly luxurious building for a wedding

111

night,' he observed. Overshadowing the square was a tall hill topped by a crumbling castle.

'It's not a particularly luxurious building,' she said as they walked through the gateway and she looked up at the white-washed stone vaulting.

In the bar room stood an enormous Italian jukebox – the only noticeable thing there apart from the brightly painted gothic ceiling. Sixteen paper roses bloomed in sixteen identical vases on sixteen tables laid for dinner. Only the table adjacent to the bar broke the pattern – long and brown, without a table-cloth. Around it were seated four men and a woman. The men, one of whom was in uniform, were drinking beer.

'Are you hungry?' he asked. He knew he was going to eat and drink slowly, for as long as possible, to delay to the utmost the moment she was also waiting for.

She looked around the room as if trying to choose which of the identical tables suited her best. Then she said, 'Shouldn't we have a wedding feast if we're on our honeymoon?'

'Why not?' he said, still playing along. 'But didn't you have a wedding feast last week?'

'No, why should I have had a wedding feast last week?' she asked in surprise.

'I thought you did,' he said, puzzled. 'After all, you did get married last week.'

'It didn't occur to me at the time,' she said. 'But there's no suitable table here.'

'They're all equally suitable,' he countered. 'We could ask them to bring a different tablecloth and different flowers, if they have them.'

'Yes,' she said, 'but where will we put the guests?'

'Guests?'

'There have to be guests at a wedding feast,' she said. 'Or don't you want to have the wedding feast here?'

'But we don't know anyone here,' he pointed out feebly.

'They don't have to be people we know. The people at that table, for instance. Maybe they'd act as guests if we invited them.'

'Okay. How many guests do you want to have at your wedding feast?'

'Five,' she answered without hesitation, as if she had made her mind up long ago. 'You're not cross, are you?'

'No, why should I be cross?'

'I bet you had a wedding feast too,' she said. 'Didn't you?'

'I don't remember any more.'

'You don't remember?'

'It was sixteen years ago,' he calculated. 'I was younger than you are now.'

He called the waiter and tried to explain to him what he wanted, while looking at the big table. Three of the men were ordinary country bumpkins. Their tanned, unshaven faces, now ruddy from drink, were the sort he was never able to recall even minutes after seeing them, even though he did not have a particularly bad memory for faces. The soldier was dark-haired and thin almost to the point of gauntness, with pale cheeks. There were bluish bags under his watery eyes. He was almost too reminiscent of that guy – the one who was now actually her husband. In fact he was reminiscent of all her lovers, to judge from her stories and the crumpled photos she always carried around in her handbag.

Sitting alongside the soldier was a girl whose hair had been recently permed by the local hairdresser. She looked like a sheep that had been given eye make-up and artificial lashes.

He watched the waiter lean over the long table. Then, as if on command, the five heads turned as one towards their table. The strangers' gaze immediately settled on her face and remained there.

He felt her touch his hand.

'Darling,' she said, 'I love you for having come on this honeymoon with me. For the wedding feast we're going to have. And for inviting them all. Look, they're coming over. Don't they look funny!'

The five of them rose from the big table and the soldier fastened his belt with a click. They approached rather hesitantly, wearing the requisite festive grins of guests coming to join the wedding party at table. He noticed that one of the old gaffers had a bluish lump under his right ear (he would forget his face but he would never forget his ear) and the girl had a fine golden chain around her bare neck.

2

The stale greasiness of the cutlet and the taste of the bad wine rose in his throat. That long car journey and now this endless evening in a room which screamed of boredom. He felt totally exhausted.

The three locals – the witnesses to their fake wedding – were endeavouring to pay for the cutlet and the wine with their lives; at least their lives offered in words. The one with the lump under his ear had spent eight years in various prisons, and the other two complemented his account as if they had gone through it all with him themselves.

He tried not to listen to them. He knew the story; it was

always the same, with slight variations. They were the very things he had hoped to avoid for this evening, at least: prisons, watchtowers, floodlights, passageways through barbed-wire. To escape from escaping.

Whenever he was with her he managed to detach himself – in retrospect, at least – from his entire life and everything he had gone through, and just sink into total amnesia, not thinking about his family or his job. He would enter a different order of cause and effect, actions and words. Maybe the overwhelming completeness of his love lay in this absolute detachment from everything he had ever lived by.

She was now dancing with the soldier to the scratchy music the Italian jukebox churned out three whole minutes of for one coin. Without looking, he knew the way she was dancing. And it had gone on too long.

He realized that her dancing had only one purpose, the same purpose as all her other actions. She made love with each of her movements. She made love when she was dancing, when she was eating and when she was walking along the pavement by herself. All her movements were the same. But maybe he was mistaken; maybe it was he who was obsessed.

'Eight years of my life,' the man with the lump said. 'I'll never make up for it at my age.' Glancing at the man, it occurred to him that they could be the same age, but the other man seemed totally immersed in his past. Those eight years had been too great a void not to exert a pull, too much of a gulf. Besides, the day comes for everyone when all that remains is their past, however awful; it alone is real and alive because the future is no longer alive, and without a glimmer of hope. He still had some hope – at that moment his hope was dancing just a few steps away – and could still imagine tomorrow without a groan of despair. But for how much longer?

For a split second he saw himself. He saw himself sitting here with weary eyes, weighed down by his whole long life, waiting. He still had something to wait for, which was why he was sitting here impatiently, waiting for the girl to finish dancing and come and sit by him.

That was where he differed from the three men sitting at his table: his life had still managed to rouse itself to a final shout before the silence that was already stealing up on him every night. It had given out a final ray before nightfall. He was in love, which was why he was sitting here playing a game, mocking himself and his love, why he was playing her game, although for her it *is* only a game, all that love, the long aimless journeys, those constant protestations that had the strange attraction of words spoken at the edge of the abyss. For her it was a way of filling the time between morning and evening, between dinner and bed, between the last cigarette and sex.

Anyone could fill that time for her, he knew. For her he was replaceable, utterly replaceable.

He looked at her. She noticed and smiled.

He could see that smile even when he closed his eyes, and her mouth with the broad, slightly protruding upper lip.

He hated her at this moment and longed to push her away from him, get rid of her, rid himself at last of that hope that was no hope, in fact, but instead wearing him out, prolonging the anxiety before the inevitable fall. Rid himself of it and sink into peace at last, reject her, reject life and the future now. But he knew he wouldn't do it.

Love me, he thought to himself wearily, love me still today, at least.

He noticed that the girl who could belong to the soldier was sitting bolt upright at the table, watching the solitary dancing couple. She was not really ugly, but that criminal of a hairdresser had ruined her hair and her face was devoid of any hint of self-assurance. Right now her eyes were full of tears.

He rose, called the waiter over and settled the bill.

The rustics stood up and wished both of them the best of luck, while the soldier stood facing her as when they stopped dancing, just a few paces nearer the table, and gazed at her with the fixed expression of a man with just one thing on his mind.

'Darling,' she said as they went upstairs, 'that was lovely. We had a feast.'

'I'm glad you were satisfied,' he said.

'What shall we do now?'

'We're on our honeymoon, aren't we?' he reminded her.

The beds were old-fashioned and the washbasin boasted two taps, although both of them ran cold.

She stood in front of the mirror removing her hair grips. Her long hair fell a third of the way down her back. He pictured her back naked, as he would soon see it. And with a sudden feeling of relief that the play-acting and the senseless hours of waiting were coming to an end, he went and put his arms around her. 'My beautiful girl,' he said. 'My little fish.'

She lit a cigarette. 'Do you think that soldier is sleeping with the girl?'

'I couldn't say,' he said brusquely. 'Soldiers generally sleep with any girl who happens to be willing.'

'So you think soldiers sleep with any girl,' she repeated.

'But she was on formal terms with him,' he recalled. 'I expect they met for the first time down there in the pub.'

She was drawing the curtains. 'He told me he works in films. In "civvy street". As a lighting technician.'

'They all work in films,' he said.

'So you think everyone works in films these days?' Only now did she look around the room. 'It's awfully cold in this room, don't you think?'

'It's a perfectly adequate room for our purposes.'

'What purposes?' she asked.

He didn't reply. He was used to not listening to her, not paying attention to her when he didn't feel like it. He just felt the distance between them.

'Are you cross, darling?' she asked.

'No,' he assured her.

'What shall we do now?' she asked.

'I don't know,' he said. 'I really don't know. I'd say it's too late for the cinema, assuming they've got a cinema here.'

'We ought to do something special,' she suggested. 'Seeing we're on our honeymoon.' She sat down on the bed. 'Tell me something. Tell me something special at least.'

'Once' – this was how he used to start stories to his children – 'when I was your age . . .'

'No,' she said, interrupting him, 'that's not what I meant. Do you love me?'

'Yes,' he replied quickly. 'You know I love you more than I've ever loved anyone.'

She said nothing. She leaned back on the pillow and half closed her eyes.

'You're my only and my last love.'

He kissed her. 'Sister of my dreams,' he said. 'Sometimes I used to wake up in the middle of the night and be afraid I'd never meet you.'

'Did you know me already?'

'No, I didn't. I wished for you. I wished for you whenever I walked down the street, whenever I got into my car, whenever I drove through a landscape I found special, nostalgic or even beautiful. And then every time I went into a hotel reception and opened the door of an empty room, every time I caught sight of a couple kissing. And I wished for you most of all when I was coming home in the summer late at night . . .'

'Hold on,' she stopped him, 'that's what you always tell me.'

'I've never told you that before!'

'I know, I know. But things like that.'

He said nothing.

'Are you cross?' she asked. 'I love it,' she said quickly. 'I love it when you say things like that to me . . . It's just that today, seeing as we're on our honeymoon . . .'

He said nothing.

'Darling,' she said, 'don't let's stay here. This is the sort of room we're always in. All we can do in it is what we always do.'

'For heaven's sake, we're planning to do what we always do, aren't we?'

'Yes . . . but today . . . today we ought to . . .' She went over to the window and drew back the curtain. Against the dark sky loomed the even darker outline of the ruined castle.

3

They could now see the hill and its castle from the other side. The dilapidated battlements were bathed in moonlight and looked majestic and threatening in the night.

He stopped the car and switched off the lights. 'Where to now?' he asked.

The night was chilly and the autumnal grass, leaves and mist gave off a scent that was almost nostalgic. It would have been quite pleasant to walk with her along this footpath through the meadow if he had felt like walking.

'The light here is weird,' she remarked. They were walking along some path that was really no more than trampled grass, his arm round her shoulders. He longed for her and hated her for it.

'Do you remember that night when we were travelling in France?' she asked.

'It was raining,' he said. 'And the path was almost impossible to walk along.'

'Yes. The rain drummed on the roof of the car.' She shivered with cold. Then she started telling a story out of the blue. 'When I was about four years old I used to pretend I had a dog. I took him on walks with a lead, as if he really existed. I would wait while he peed against a tree and I'd always put something from my dinner plate into a bowl for him. I used to make up a bed for him out of a cushion beside my own bed and pretend he was lying there. And every night before I went to sleep I would talk to him. I never gave him a name, I just used to call him "my dog".' She sighed. 'I don't think I ever loved anyone as much as that dog.'

They had reached a wooden hut in the middle of the meadow. From within came the scent of hay.

'Come on, darling,' she said, 'let's make love now.'

He helped her climb up.

The space inside was half filled with hay and the air was stiflingly thick with hay dust.

'Darling,' she whispered, 'do you like it here?'

'I don't care where I am when I'm with you,' he said.

'Yes, I know,' she said, quickly undressing, 'but it couldn't have been in a bedroom today. You're not cross with me because of it, are you?' She pressed herself to him. He put his arms around her. With every movement they sunk deeper into the soft stuff beneath them and the stalks tickled and pricked their naked bodies.

'Darling,' she whispered.

From outside came the sound of footsteps. He raised himself and made out a familiar shape.

'So this is the place, then?' the soldier asked after they had climbed up.

'If you like it here,' the girl whispered. Her face and even her hairstyle were now hidden in the darkness. The soldier had laid his belt aside ceremoniously the moment he arrived as if loath to make any unnecessary movements.

'You're so handsome,' the girl whispered.

He seemed to be kissing her. All they could hear were short breaths, drunken wheezing, the sound of groping hands, the crackle of the straw and then the girl's moaning whisper, 'Don't worry about me, don't worry about me, just so long as you're satisfied.'

A few minutes later, as silence suddenly fell, the soldier stood up and tried to read the time from his watch by the light of the moon.

'Do you want to go already?' the girl whispered.

'It's almost midnight,' the soldier said ruefully. 'Why didn't you tell me earlier about this hayloft?' He spat. Maybe it was only to spit out straw from his mouth. He snapped his belt on again and the two of them climbed down into the darkness almost without a sound.

'Darling,' she whispered when they were alone once more, 'do you love me?'

He tried to make out her face in the dark, but it was so indistinct it could have been any face. Moreover, the scent of her body was smothered by the irritating stench of hay.

'No,' he said. And he thought to himself, I hate you. Because you make a game out of what for me is love and because you are my only and final future while for you I am simply a moment that's already passing.

'No,' she repeated after him. 'He doesn't love me.'

He remained silent. If only he were fifteen years younger.

'He simply doesn't love me any more,' she said. 'Why?'

'Because you're . . .' but he didn't continue.

'Because I'm a whore?' she asked.

He said nothing.

'So you went off on a honeymoon with a whore?' She cuddled up to him. 'My love,' she kissed him. He held her in his arms.

'At last, at last,' she whispered. 'At last.'

'I love you,' he said. 'I love you madly and I'd give everything, absolutely everything for this moment with you.'

'I know,' she whispered. 'I know. Dog,' she then said quietly. 'My dog!'

(1969)

122

Intimate Conversations

LONG-DISTANCE CONVERSATIONS

'This is Wellington, New Zealand. Is that Prague? Hold the line for a call.'

'Hello. Hello. Is that Prague?'

'This is Prague here.'

'Is that you, Tereza? Can you hear me?'

'Yes, I can hear you.'

'It's me. Bill.'

'I know. I recognized your voice. And who else would call me from there?'

'How are you, Tereza?'

'Fine now that I can hear you. Can you hear me? How are you?'

'It's good to hear you. But you sound terribly distant.'

'I know. I'm on the other side of the world.'

'I miss you, Tereza!'

'I miss you, too.'

'I wish I could hold you.'

'Me too.'

'What's the news?'

'I'm not sure. None really. The older boy is going to school now and the little one is wrecking the flat and my nerves. I've got loads of work. I'm having a new outfit made. I thought about you when I had the fitting, wondering if you'd like me in it. And how about you?'

'Tereza, I told my wife everything.'

'What's everything?'

'That I love you.'

'You told her about me?'

'I told her I'm in love with you and want to live with you. Didn't you tell your husband?'

'No . . . Not yet. Do you think that was wise? What did she say?'

'She didn't believe me at first. And then – she cried.'

'That's terrible. Perhaps you should have waited a little longer. Hello? Hello . . . Are you there? I can't hear you, Bill. There's somebody talking Japanese or something on the line. Are you still there?'

'Tereza, can you hear me?'

'Now I can. It's awful, the distance.'

'Unbearable. That wasn't Japanese, that was Maori. I don't see what I'm supposed to wait for – I know I love you.'

'Now I can hear you as if you were in the next room. But it must have hurt her terribly.'

'It's not the telling that hurt her but what happened. And what's going to happen.'

'It's all awful. And what are you going to do? What have you agreed with your wife?'

'It wasn't easy. She told me she might not survive. I need to talk to you about it.'

'Do you mean over the phone, interrupted by someone talking Maori all the time? Surely we can't talk about life and death matters over the phone?'

'Exactly. I wanted to tell you I've decided to fly out to see you.'

'That's out of the question.'

'Why? I'd take the plane, that's all. Like last month.'

'But it costs so much.'

'I don't care about the money. I only care about being with you.'

'How could you be with me? I have my husband here, don't forget.'

'And you did last month too.'

'Yes, but he wasn't here. He was away.'

'But I expect you could find a moment for me.'

'A moment perhaps. And you'd fly all the way for that?'

'I'd sooner have a moment with you than a life without you. Besides, we need to take some decisions. And you said yourself that these decisions can't be taken over the telephone.'

'But you were only here a month ago. We could have taken decisions then but we didn't.'

'We didn't because there wasn't the time. And I didn't realize then how dreadful life would be without you.'

'But we talked about that too, didn't we? About how we'd miss each other. And you told me you wouldn't put me under pressure, that I was to take my time and decide for myself.'

'But of course you must be free to make up your own mind. That goes without saying.'

'There you are, then.'

'It would never occur to me to put you under any sort of pressure.'

'That's okay then. But you want me to come over there and live with you. And I can't. And I don't want to either. I can hardly be expected to leave now after staying through all the rotten Communist years? I happen to like this country. And my family's here.'

'But I've never tried to force you.'

'No, you haven't. But what other hope do we have of living together? After all, you can't fly back and forth every month.'

'Why not? Anyway, I've come up with another solution apart from flying back and forth.'

'What solution?'

'Sweetheart, I've decided to move over there.'

'To Czechia?'

'To your country. What exactly is it called now?'

'Czechia. Czecho, if you like. It makes no difference. But that's insane. What job would you do here? We've no sea.'

'That doesn't matter.'

'What do you mean, it doesn't matter? You're a naval officer and we don't have any ships.'

'Yes you do, as a matter of fact. I made enquiries. You've got five ships.'

'But those ships are out at sea six months at a time.'

'Not quite so long. And ships are always at sea.'

'But I wouldn't see you for six months at a time.'

'If I stay here I'll have to fly back and forth or you wouldn't see me either.'

'I know.'

'But I thought you told me you wanted to be with me always.'

'I did, I do. You're so far away, though. And your wife and your little daughters are there. And I'm married.'

'That's why I want to move over there. After all, there must be some way of working it out so that the two of us can be together.'

'But your career is with the navy.'

'I wouldn't have to find a job at sea. I could earn my living some other way. I could drive a taxi perhaps. Besides, you've got river navigation.'

'You want to re-train to take care of a raft?'

'As a matter of fact they've got some rather nice little steamers. And they'd have a job for me starting in September.'

'The fact that you're a sea captain was one of the things that appealed to me most about you.'

'That's another thing I need to talk to you about. We've got manoeuvres in September.'

'And you'll be in command.'

'Something like that.'

'That must be fascinating.'

'That's not the point right now. But I can hardly give them just one week's notice that I'm going.'

'Where to?'

'I told you. I'll have a job with that navigation company of yours from September onwards.'

'But it's only June now.'

'Exactly. It's June already. Which means I'd have to give my notice in straight away.'

'But you couldn't, could you, not with those manoeuvres?'

'I could, but I'd have to let them know before the end of the week.'

'And you want to hear from me by the end of the week whether you should come over?'

'I need to know, in order to make my decision.'

'But you promised me you'd give me time to make up my own mind.'

'Naturally. I can't force you, can I?'

'But you're forcing me now!'

'What am I forcing you to do?'

'Hello, Bill, can you hear me? There's someone talking in Maori again. Can you hear me?'

'Yes, I can hear you, and that blithering idiot too. That's no Maori, that's Japanese.'

'What's he saying?'

'Who?'

'The man talking Japanese.'

'It's not important. To hell with him. He says it looks like margarine prices are going to fall. He's talking about the Dow Jones index.'

'I can hear you fine now. The margarine man has disappeared. What were we saying?'

'That you have to be free to make up your own mind. I'd never put you under any pressure. You're a free woman, Tereza. With me you'd be free at last. I just need to know whether I'm to withdraw from those manoeuvres.'

'Exchange here. Is that seven one zero, eight one three?'

'Hang on! What did you say? Lord, I can't even remember my own number now.'

'It's all right, I recognize your voice. You've got Wellington on the line again.'

'Tereza?'

'Yes, Bill.'

'Are you alone?'

'Yes. There's only my little boy with me.'

'Tereza, it'll soon be Friday here.'

'Not here though. It's only Thursday morning.'

'I realize that. But I'll have to give my reply today.'

'About those manoeuvres?'

'About whether I'm going to leave the navy.'

'But you always told me that it was your business what you did.'

'Naturally. I just wanted to know if you agreed with me that I should leave.'

'The navy, or New Zealand?'

'The one depends on the other.'

'But Bill, I was trying to tell you last time. You have your family there. What will become of them?'

'My family would stay where they are now.'

'You'd leave your little girls there?'

'Tereza, I love you. I can't live without you. What am I to do? I have to give up something, or someone. I've already told them.'

'You've told them you're leaving and coming here?'

'I told my wife.'

'And how about her?'

'I've already told you. First she said she wouldn't get over it. Then she said I was off my head.'

'Stop that, for heaven's sake!'

'What did you say?'

'It's awful. My little monster has tipped salt into the sugar bowl.'

'That's not important, is it?'

'I didn't say it was important. Listen, do you really want to live here?'

'I've already found a job there.'

'Have you accepted it yet?'

'No, I've just discussed it with them. And I've already started learning Czech.'

'You really are crazy.'

'Yes, about you, sweetheart.'

'But, Bill, you promised me, you said you'd let me have time . . .'

'You can have all you want, but I have to give them a reply.'

'Because of those rafts?'

'They're quite nice little steamers.'

'When do you have to give your answer?'

'Soon. And the people here today. Or by next week at the latest.'

'But we can't come to any agreement over the phone, can we?'

'And that's precisely the reason I told you last time I wanted to come over. Don't you agree?'

'I'm not sure. Anyway I told you I'm here with my husband and the children.'

'I'm aware of that, aren't I? I'd get on fine with your kids.'

'Stay out of here, for God's sake!'

'What did you say?'

'It's my little one. He's trying to climb into the oven when it's switched on. And what about my husband?'

'You told me, if I'm not mistaken, that you have a dog's life with him.'

'Bill, that's something we can't solve over the phone. And it costs a fortune.'

'I don't care about the money. I care about you.'

'I care about you too.'

'I love you. And I can already say it to you in Czech. *Milovávám tě na celou duši.* Did I get it right?'

'Not quite, Bill. But I understand you. And I love you too. *Z celé duše.*'

'There you go.'

'And that's precisely the reason I don't want you to do something you'll regret later. Something that will drive us both to despair.'

'I'll never regret it so long as I'm with you. I'd only despair if I had to live without you.'

'And without your little girls?'

'They'll grow up all the same. And they'll be married in a few years' time.'

'How can you talk about your own children that way? They're still only little. You have to live for the present, for heaven's sake. You can't act according to what might or might not happen.'

'Tereza, don't you love me any more?'

'Wellington here. Are you still talking, Prague?'

'Yes we are, but we're nearly finished.'

'We're nearly finished, Tereza?'

'But it's costing you a fortune.'

'No, I thought you meant finished with me. You haven't told me if you still love me.'

'I love you as much as ever.'

'Do you remember the first time we met?'

'Yes, but we can scarcely talk about it at such a distance, can we?'

'You told me I was the sort of man you could spend your life with.'

'Yes, because you're calm and kind, and you love me. You were nice to my parents when I introduced you to them last time you were here. My husband quarrels with them. He quarrels with everyone, in fact, because he only sees people's bad sides. And I was very attracted to you. My sea captain. You'll take command at the manoeuvres.'

'I won't. I'll live over there in your country. That's what I need us to agree on.'

'But Bill, everything's different here. And there's no sea.'

'I've had enough of the sea. You're what's special for me.'

'Because you have the sea all around you, but you don't have me. If you come here, you'll have me right enough, but you'll start to miss the sea.'

'How can you compare yourself to the sea? The sea is water and you're fire.'

'Darling, you say such beautiful things to me, but we must finish. We'll never sort it out over the phone, anyway.'

'You haven't told me yet whether you want me to come over.'

'What I want isn't the point. It wouldn't be sensible.'

'Why wouldn't it be sensible? We miss each other so much and we have to take decisions about our future.'

'Because we have our families. After all, you said I have to be absolutely free to decide.'

'Of course. I can't make you do anything, can I?'

'How can I be free to decide if you come over here and tell me you'll leave your family and your country because of me, and then you'll ruin these manoeuvres. Are they important?'

'Who?'

'The manoeuvres.'

'The biggest for ten years.'

'There you are. And you'd go and miss them.'

'That's my affair.'

'No, it isn't just your affair. If you give up your job and

abandon everything on account of me how am I supposed to be free to decide? Don't you realize what a responsibility this places on me? After all, I can't even be sure that you'd be happy with me.'

'With you I'll be happy. And you yourself said how nice it would be if we could be together all the time.'

'I said it because I love you.'

'There you are, then.'

'But at the same time I knew you were a long way away and that it could never come true. If you were nearer everything would be easier, and we could get to know each other better as well. We've hardly known each other for more than a couple of weeks.'

'Times two.'

'Yes. But that first time, when we met at the seaside, we had no idea that we'd fall in love.'

'I knew it the first time I saw you.'

'We didn't know it for certain. We were both on holiday. And when you're on holiday everything seems different and special.'

'It was special. But I knew I could never meet another woman like you.'

'What sort of woman am I?'

'Remarkable. Beautiful. Delicate. Tender. Wise.'

'Bill, you wrote and told me all that before. Don't waste time now. We've been talking for so long already. This phone call will cost you more than the plane ticket.'

'Don't think about the cost of the call and tell me whether I ought to fly over.'

'This is the Wellington operator. Are you still speaking, Prague?'

'This is Bill Morgan here, also in Wellington. What the hell do you keep butting in like that for?'

'Excuse me, sir, but I had the feeling your call was a trifle long.'

'There's no need for you to worry yourself about the length of our call. You're not paying!'

'Bill, I don't think you should come. I'm not sure I'll have the time or the chance to meet you. My husband always wants to know what I do during the day . . .'

'Tell him you're going to your parents'. We could meet there.'

'Oh, for Pete's sake, pack that in! Turn that tap off right away!'

'What's that?'

'Nothing. I wasn't talking to you.'

'Is someone there with you?'

'I told you already. My little boy. Now he's gone and tipped flour in the sink and is running the water. What were we saying?'

'That we could meet at your parents'.'

'I'm not sure I want to drag them into it. Oh Jesus, the flour's blocked the waste pipe. Bill, I'm sorry, I can't concentrate, the sink's overflowing. And anyway you promised me time to think it over!'

'Seven one zero eight one three? I have that gentleman from Wellington for you again.'

'Tereza, it's Friday here now. Are you there on your own?'

'Yes. My little boy has just gone to sleep.'

'That's good. At least we'll have a bit of peace and time for ourselves.'

'But Bill, what do you mean by time? You only called three hours ago.'

'Precisely. You've had a chance to think it over.'

'What can I have thought over?'

'Whether I'm to fly there. That's not a very tough decision, is it?'

'But Bill, I can't even be sure we'll be able to meet. I told you I didn't want to drag my parents into it.'

'How about some girlfriend?'

'I don't know, Bill. Girlfriends are out too.'

'Think up something else, then. Otherwise just tell him I've arrived and we need to talk to each other.'

'Do you think I ought to tell him everything about you?'

'It would be the honourable thing.'

'But he might kill you. Or me. Or himself. You don't know him.'

'You see the kind of life you have with him!'

'Would you put up with it if I was your wife and told you someone else – my lover – was flying in to see me?'

'I wouldn't kill anyone. At the most I'd chuck him in the sea and let him sink or swim.'

'But there's no sea here, Bill!'

'So I'd chuck him in any old water.'

'You're different, I know. That's why I fell in love with you.'

'And do you love him too, seeing that you're always so concerned about him?'

'I'm not talking about love. But he is still my husband after all.'

'I thought you didn't love him any more. That you didn't want to live with him. So why are you so concerned about him?'

'That's true. But he's terribly attached to the children.'

'But you wouldn't be taking them from him.'

'And the children are attached to him. He's their father.'

'You said you're always having terrible rows at home. That he yells at them needlessly. That he makes them neurotic.'

'We do have rows sometimes. Awful ones. We hurl the crockery at each other in the kitchen. Sometimes he yells at the boys. And twice he wanted to kill himself. Now I can hear some music on the line. What absurd kind of music is that anyway? Some Chinese thing or other. Can you hear me at all? It's enough to drive you mad.'

'There you are. It's enough to drive you mad.'

'What is?'

'Life with your husband.'

'That as well. But at this moment it's the telephone. I can hear you again. What was I talking about?'

'Your husband. How he wanted to kill you on two occasions.'

'Not me. He wanted to kill himself.'

'Sorry, I misheard you. There was some Maori band on the line. He wanted to kill himself on account of you?'

'He wanted to kill himself in a rage. Or from despair. Or maybe it was just a threat. He wants to bind me to him, to make me obedient and faithful.'

'Do you think that's good for the children?'

'It certainly isn't.'

'There you are.'

'But we don't quarrel all the time. Sometimes our home is quite peaceful. And he plays with them and reads them Bible stories and tries to bring them up as decent people.'

'I'd read them Bible stories too. We always read the Bible at home on Sundays.'

'In your home?'

'Yes, in my home.'

'And tell me, could you really leave it behind? Don't you love your home?'

'I love you. My home will be wherever you are.'

'How can you tell?'

'I just feel it.'

'This is a foreign country.'

'My ancestors also came to a foreign country. Everyone here bar the Maoris came to a totally foreign country. The journey by ship could take three months in those days. And even the Maoris haven't always been here.'

'But you were born there. You have your parents, your brother, your friends, your wife, your children and the sea.'

'But I haven't got you.'

'Do you mean to say that I count for more than everything else?'

'Yes, that's just what I mean to say.'

'But you hardly know me. After a couple of months here you might start to regret it.'

'I never regret anything I do.'

'You married once and now you want to go away and leave them. And you don't regret it?'

'No. We loved each other once and then it ended. I don't regret it.'

'You'll love me and then it'll end. Won't you regret it?'

'It won't end!'

'If it ended, would you regret it?'

'It won't end.'

'But if it ended you would regret it.'

'No, I wouldn't.'

LOVERS FOR A DAY

'What would you find to do here in a foreign country? A
sailor with no sea. A man with no home, no family, no friends?'

'Didn't you tell me just a while ago that one has to live for
the present and not act in terms of what will or won't happen?'

'But we'd break up our families. Both you and I.'

'They're broken already. After what has happened.'

'But things like that happen in life and the family doesn't
have to break up on account of them.'

'When love ends it never returns.'

'Are you so sure?'

'I'm speaking about myself.'

'Bill, these phone calls must have cost the price of an air
ticket already. You might as well have come straight here.'

'You didn't tell me whether I should come.'

'I'm really not sure, Bill. It'd be awfully complicated.'

'Life is complicated. Until the day you die.'

'But some complications are needless. Or excessive.'

'Do you think I'm an excessive complication?'

'No, not you. You're someone who's very dear to me.'

'So why don't you want me to come?'

'Hello, Bill, are you there? You keep fading away.'

'What did you say?'

'I said you're fading away.'

'There you are. That's something I know from the sea. First
your country fades away and then everything else. Even the
ones you love the most. Otherwise you'd go mad.'

'What would make you go mad?'

'Getting up every morning and knowing all you'll see that
day is the sea and none of your loved ones, the ones that make
your life worth living. That's why I want to come to you.'

'Don't come, Bill!'

'You tell me not to come, even though I'm fading from your life?'

'I was only talking about the phone. Otherwise you're not. I mean, I'm not sure. Bill, to come all this way, when we're not even sure we'll be able to meet? The whole thing is madness. I realize I ought to have thought better of it before, but I fell in love with you. Now I'm frightened of the consequences. Not just for me, but for you too. I'm touched by what you want to do and I love you for it. But at the same time I'm afraid.'

'One should only be afraid of dying.'

'Don't talk about dying.'

'Living without you seems to me like dying.'

'That's blasphemy!'

'A day without you is like the sea without dry land. There's nowhere to come back to, nothing to look forward to.'

'Bill, you're a . . . a . . . I don't know how to say it in English.'

'Say it in Czech then.'

'You're a *cvok*.'

'What's a *cvok*?'

'That's the problem! I don't know how to explain it. It means you're crazy in a nice sort of way.'

'I'm not crazy. I just know what I want. And now finally tell me if I should come!'

'I'm not sure, Bill. I'd love to see you, but at the same time I'm afraid of not finding a solution. Of assuming the responsibility. Wait a moment, someone's opening the front door. My husband's coming in. Quick, say something important. Just the most important thing.'

'Okay. I've got to see you or I'll die. I'll arrive there next

Wednesday via London. At one-thirty p.m. I've already bought my ticket. Do you love me?'

'Yes.'

'I love you – like a *cvok*. I can't wait to see you.'

'This is Wellington. Are you still speaking?'

'No, not any more, thank you!'

'God, I'm hungry. I've been on the go non-stop since this morning and didn't find a moment for lunch. Have you got something for dinner?'

'Yes, of course . . . I'll fix you a sandwich in a moment.'

'Is something up?'

'No, why should there be?'

'You were on the phone when I came in.'

'It was nothing . . . nothing important.'

'It's okay, you look a bit worked up, that's all.'

'What do you mean?'

'You seem a bit jumpy.'

'No, I'm not. I was talking with my dressmaker, that's all.'

'What did she want?'

'She told me the outfit she's making for me will be ready soon. I'm to pick it up on Wednesday at one-thirty.'

'You've had another outfit made?'

'Yes. I have to dress nicely. So you'll find me attractive!'

(1994)

CONJUGAL CONVERSATIONS

'I'd like to talk to you.'

'Now?'

'Now or very soon.'

'You say it so seriously.'

'I'm saying it quite normally.'

'I was planning to do something.'

'You are always planning to do something. Anything not to have to talk to me.'

'I was planning to oil the door hinges. They creak horribly. And aren't we always talking?'

'That depends what you mean by talking.'

'Talking means opening one's mouth and saying words.'

'Yes, that's precisely what you do mean by talking.'

'Do you have a better definition?'

'I'm not interested in definitions, I'm interested in having a conversation.'

'Okay: converse.'

'I would like us both to converse.'

'You start, then.'

'How can I start when you won't even sit down. You're standing there in the doorway looking for an excuse to dash away.'

'Sorry. I'm listening now.'

'It's ages since we spent a whole evening together.'

'How do you mean?'

'I mean a proper family evening together, the two of us and the children.'

'But we're together every evening, aren't we?'

'Really? When was the last time?'

'Yesterday, for instance.'

'Yesterday evening you came home at nine-thirty. You'd had an important meeting. Or so you said.'

'What's that supposed to mean, "Or so you said"?'

'It means that yesterday we weren't together.'

'Sorry, but yesterday I really did have a departmental meeting. And it was on a fairly important matter. Namely, funding for the whole year.'

'And the day before was a club night.'

'I only have one club night a month.'

'Sunday evening you were playing tennis. On Saturday you watched television. And before that you came home a couple of times when the children were already asleep.'

'Are you keeping tabs on my movements?'

'No, I just remember because it upsets me, and the children too.'

'Okay, I'll give up tennis.'

'I don't want you to give up tennis. I want you to feel the need to be here with us sometimes.'

'How can you tell me what needs I ought to be feeling?'

144

'You don't think I should want anything from you?'

'You can want anything you like from me, but don't tell me what my needs should be.'

'Sorry. It's just that it upsets me that you act as if you don't need us.'

'I do need you. After all, everything I do, I do for you.'

'That's only an excuse. Just to make you look magnanimous in your own eyes.'

'I don't need to look magnanimous in my own eyes. Or in anyone else's, for that matter. But you can hardly deny that I look after you.'

'That's not the point.'

'I'm not really sure what the point is.'

'The point is that it's ages since we spent a proper evening together.'

'And don't you think I might just like one too? It's not my fault I have so little spare time.'

'Whose fault is it, then?'

'I don't know. It's just the way things are. If you hesitate for a second, there's someone stealing a march on you.'

'At work, you mean?'

'Yes, at work. In research.'

'And elsewhere?'

'What do you mean by elsewhere?'

'At home, for instance.'

'Here, do you mean?'

'I wasn't aware you had a home somewhere else.'

'That's an interesting thought.'

'It's never occurred to you before, then?'

'That someone might steal a march on me here? Who, for instance?'

'It wouldn't be too hard to find someone.'

'And you have someone in mind?'

'No, I used to think I had you.'

'And you don't any more?'

'I'm not sure now. I don't know whether I've got you. I've got the money you bring home and the dishes you make dirty, and the shirts that I wash for you.'

'I thought the washing machine did that.'

'I don't want to talk about shirts, I want to talk about us.'

'You're the one who mentioned the shirts.'

'I was only asking what we get from you, the children and me.'

'The children don't wash shirts.'

'The children don't even get dirty shirts from you.'

'You act as if I ignored the children.'

'Would you mind telling me, then, when we last spent a family evening together?'

'And what's this "family evening" supposed to consist of, for heaven's sake?'

'Sitting around the table for a meal and chatting together.'

'Chatting about what?'

'What we've been doing during the day, for instance. Or what we've been reading.'

'Economic analyses and statistics are what I read most of the time. I shouldn't think they'd interest you.'

'You could hear about what the children or I have been reading. If you're at all interested.'

'Your idea of a family evening sounds a bit like school. Questions about what you read for homework.'

'We wouldn't have to talk about books. You could explain to us what your work's about. Or what you want from life. Or what we are doing here.'

'You really think that would interest them? The boy's into model-making and the girl's into clothes and the absurd pop songs she stares at on television.'

'You didn't teach them anything better, did you?'

'So I'm to blame for that too, am I?'

'It's not a question of blame.'

'Why don't you find them something better to do, then?'

'Perhaps I've tried, but it's been too much for me on my own.'

'In other words, you're all on your own.'

'It feels like that sometimes. I've always been left to deal with things like that on my own. The most you were ever up to was helping the boy stick his models together.'

'I'd sooner have him sticking models than trailing round the pubs in a gang.'

'But one day they'll want to start their own families and they'll look back on their childhood.'

'Do you think it'll strike them as so awful? What have they lacked?'

'Nothing apart from the fact they won't be able to recall a single proper family evening.'

'Not one? What about Christmas?'

'Christmas in our home is an orgy of present-giving. You always try and make up for what we don't get from you at other times.'

'It never occurred to me that I should regard myself as the one who owed anything on that score. And I never got the impression things like that bothered you particularly. Think of all the time you spend at that dressmaker's every month.'

'I haven't been to see my dressmaker for at least six months. But I'm not complaining about what I have to wear. We're not talking about material things, are we? We're talking about the time we spend together as a family?'

'Why the "we"? I'm fairly happy with my evenings. And I think the children can look back on lots of nice evenings.'

'Can you really recall a single one? When we were all here together? Just one?'

'Stop interrogating me. You're not in the classroom now. And stop looking as if you were on the verge of tears.'

'How am I supposed to look when I am on the verge of tears?'

'You're the last person to have a reason to cry. Tell me what's missing from your life.'

'I'm sorry you can't sense it.'

'You're right. I'm insensitive. It's a pity you didn't pick someone more sensitive. Someone who'd lay on nice evenings for you. Some poet or other who'd recite his work to you. Stop crying. For my part, I'm sorry you don't realize that everything I do, I do so we can live half decently.'

'But we're not talking about that at all.'

'No, we're talking about nice evenings chatting together. Like now, for instance. This evening strikes me as going really well. We'll look back on this as a really successful one.'

'What's up? Why don't you come to bed?'

'Wait a second. I'll be right there. I have to wash, don't I?'

'You always take ages. Sometimes I think you deliberately drag it out because you know I'm tired. You hope I'll fall asleep in the meantime.'

'Don't you think I'm tired as well? These few minutes in the bathroom is the only time I have to myself all day. And no sooner am I out than you pounce on me like a vulture.'

'That's not a very apt comparison.'

'Why not?'

'Because vultures pounce on corpses.'

'Are you trying to say I'm like a corpse?'

'It was your idea. The vulture.'

'You're disgusting.'

'Don't keep me waiting any more, then.'

'After what you just called me? No one could blame me if I did act like a corpse.'

'I know you've had a hard day of it.'

'It's not so much what I have to do during the day as the fact that you ignore me the whole day and then want me to make love to you.'

'What do you mean I ignore you the whole day? I'm at the university the whole day.'

'There was a time when you'd phone me, at least.'

'You mean I don't phone you now?'

'Only when you need something.'

'Fine. Tomorrow I'll make a point of calling you. First thing. But at this moment I happen to be here.'

'I couldn't care less about the telephone. But at least if you'd hold me a bit first. Or say something loving to me.'

'Don't I ever say loving things to you?'

'Most of the time you don't say anything. When we were going out together – do you remember? In those days you used to say all sorts of nice things. You used to call me your little pussy cat.'

'Yes, I liked the pussy cat one. I thought it had a nice ambiguity.'

'That never occurred to me, I must say. And there was I thinking you meant I had claws.'

'You never struck me as having claws.'

'A woman is what a man makes her. Anyway you used to jump on me wherever we went. In the woods or the park. And once, out in the yard behind the bins, remember? I told you you were off your head, that someone would see us.'

'But it was pitch dark.'

'It may have been dark, but it stank of garbage. That didn't worry you, though, your mind was on one thing.'

'I wanted you. I was crazy about you.'

'Yes. And each time you'd tell me you loved me over and over again. You never stopped saying it in those days, and now you grab me without a word. You act like an animal.'

'I can hardly go on telling you I love you for fifteen years, can I?'

'Why not, if you love me?'

'I'd feel like a parrot. Or a robot. Repeating the same sentence over and over again.'

'You don't seem to mind acting like a robot and doing the same thing over and over again.'

'What am I then – a robot or an animal?'

'You act like a programmed animal.'

'Thank you. That's something you wouldn't have said fifteen years ago.'

'Because you used to act differently. Or you used to tell me you loved me in those days. And I hadn't heard of programming then.'

'Okay. So I'll tell you I love you.'

'I don't want you to tell me, I want you to love me.'

'But that's hardly something you can ask of me, is it?'

'Don't you love me any more then?'

'I didn't say that.'

'But you don't, do you? I'm only good for one thing.'

'It seems you're not even good for that, are you?'

'You're vile. You always were. And you only called me pussy because it sounded dirty. And it never even occurred to me at the time.'

'There was nothing wrong with the fact that I wanted every part of you.'

'Did you want me then?'

'Of course, I still do.'

'I don't only mean just below the waist.'

'I still want all of you.'

'There was only one side of me you were ever really interested in. The rest you regarded as a sort of necessary evil.'

'What do you mean by the rest?'

'The fact I had a soul. Or feelings, seeing that you don't believe in the soul.'

'I've always tried to respect them.'

'Not my feelings, you haven't. You've only thought about yourself. You know that full well.'

'What do I know full well?'

'No one has ever hurt me the way you did.'

'Me? When did I hurt you?'

'The time you didn't take precautions and you bullied me into having an abortion. Or have you forgotten?'

'But you didn't have it.'

'No, I didn't. Because I'd never do anything like that. But you wanted me to. You wanted to kill our little boy.'

'Our little boy is now fifteen and he's thriving.'

'Agreed. But you wanted me to have him killed.'

'I didn't force you into anything, did I. I simply thought the time wasn't yet right for children. Anyway, the boy's alive, so what's the point of talking about it?'

'Only thanks to me. You would have had him murdered. And me along with him.'

'If he hadn't lived, another one would have.'

'How dare you say that to me? Get out! Get out of my sight!'

'Sorry, I didn't mean it that way. Even at the time.'

'You did. You disgusting creature.'

'I see. So I'm a vulture, whereas you're a . . .'

'Yes, you are a vulture. And you're doing your best to make a corpse of me.'

'I notice you're hardly in the door and you're already singing to yourself.'

'Why shouldn't I sing if I'm in a good mood?'

'You're in a good mood, then? I'm glad to hear it. What brought that on?'

'Not you, that's for sure!'

'That's obvious, seeing you've spent the day God knows where.'

'Yes, God knows, and you don't. That's what bugs you, doesn't it? Had supper already?'

'I had a slice of bread.'

'Did you butter it at least?'

'I didn't eat it dry.'

'How about the children?'

'I gave them some bread too. Buttered.'

'What else?'

'You're very curious all of a sudden. Why didn't you come and see to it yourself?'

'I'm glad you gave them their supper.'

'For the fourth time this week.'

'Is that a fact? But you told me to have the week off. It was your idea.'

'The reason I suggested it was because I couldn't stand to hear you moaning about how you sacrifice yourself for us any longer.'

'It was a nice gesture.'

'Have a good time today?'

'Splendid, thank you.'

'May I ask with whom?'

'You may. But I don't have to reply, do I?'

'It is the polite thing to reply when someone asks a question.'

'And you're someone, all of a sudden?'

'Who am I then?'

'You're my darling heart.'

'You can't mean me.'

'There's no one else here, is there?'

'I can't see anyone, but maybe in your mind's eye you can see someone else in my place.'

'I see you. You smile at me nicely, you've given the children their supper and you're even interested in who I spent the afternoon with.'

'And the evening.'

'The evening's now, with you.'

'The evening began a good while ago.'

'Could you tell me when exactly? I have to admit I'm never really sure when the evening actually begins.'

'Six o'clock, say.'

'Even now in the summer?'

'Six o'clock is the time for the family to come together.'

'So that's why you are always home on the stroke of six.'

'Whenever I'm able, I'm here. And you've not answered my question.'

'Did you ask me something?'

'You know very well what I asked you.'

'I'm afraid I've forgotten.'

'I see you don't intend to answer. That's an answer too. Aren't you even going to kiss me?'

'Of course I am, my darling.'

'Have you been drinking?'

'No. I had a glass of wine with Olga.'

'Olga who?'

'I thought you asked me who I spent the afternoon with.'

'And the evening.'

'Now I'm with you. And you know who Olga is, don't you? I must have mentioned her at least a hundred times. But then my girlfriends never did interest you, did they?'

'It's you I'm interested in, not your girlfriends.'

'You ought to know that girlfriends are part of every woman's life.'

'Wherever did you come across that bit of wisdom? You really have been drinking!'

'I've had a glass of wine.'

'Or two.'

'Or two.'

'How many?'

'I don't keep count of things like you do, my darling.'

'You're telling me. But I suppose you noticed how much you had to pay at the end. Or didn't you pay the bill?'

'Of course I paid for myself. I'd hardly let Olga pay for me.'

'That's assuming there was only Olga.'

'Do you think I'm lying to you?'

'I'm not saying you're lying to me. You told me you were with Olga, but that doesn't mean you two were alone, does it?'

'Oh, you're such a precise and logical thinker.'

'Would you mind answering then?'

'Did you ask me something?'

'I asked you if there was someone else there apart from Olga.'

'So that was a question, was it? Do men interest you, or only women?'

'What's that supposed to mean?'

'Whether you're interested in men as well as women?'

'What interests me is who you've been spending all afternoon and evening with while your family have been waiting at home for you.'

'There were about twenty people in the place. But we had a table to ourselves. There was one rather nice-looking, dark-haired man who came and asked if he could join us, but we refused him politely.'

'Who refused him?'

'I don't recall. Me, or Olga.'

'While we're on the subject of dark-haired men – this is a little embarrassing – but today my assistant told me that he saw you on Monday with a dark-haired chap.'

'According to you your assistant's a fool.'

'He may be a fool, but he's not blind.'

'I didn't say he was. Where and when did he see me?

'On Monday, at the bottom of Wenceslas Square.'

'Monday's a long day.'

'Monday's as long a day as any other and I assume you

don't spend the whole day in Wenceslas Square.'

'Ah, now I remember. It was Vašek. We just happened to bump into each other.'

'Who's Vašek?'

'A college friend.'

'What would a college friend of yours be doing at the bottom of Wenceslas Square?'

'Why shouldn't he be there? Do you think my college pals are banned from the bottom of Wenceslas Square on Mondays or something?'

'I was always under the impression you went to college in Kolín.'

'But darling, most of my fellow students moved to Prague ages ago.'

'What does he do, this Vašek?'

'You're jealous, my darling.'

'I'm not, and stop calling me darling, when you'd sooner bite me.'

'Darling, you may not even be aware of it, but you really are jealous!'

'I'm not. I just don't intend to be made a total fool of.'

'No, your assistant's the fool.'

'Why didn't you tell me about this Vašek?'

'You didn't ask.'

'How could I ask when you didn't tell me you just happened to bump into him?'

'Why the stress on the words "bump into"?'

'It's just that it really does strike me as an extraordinary coin-cidence that you should bump into a college friend from Kolín at the bottom of Wenceslas Square at half past ten on a Monday morning.'

'Your assistant may be a fool, but he has a good idea of the time.'

'My assistant isn't such a fool. Maybe I'm a bigger one. How come you were at the bottom of Wenceslas Square at that time?'

'On Mondays I have a free period from ten to twelve. I thought you knew my timetable.'

'You've never felt the need to communicate it to me.'

'I don't expect you were interested. Besides, it's always changing.'

'Besides which it suits you that I don't know your free periods. But you haven't told me yet why you never mentioned him to me.'

'I suppose that evening as usual you didn't have time to talk. And anyway it never occurred to me you'd be interested in any of my old college friends.'

'What interests me is who you spend your time with. That's quite normal, I would have thought.'

'You mustn't be jealous, darling. You know you're the only one I have. Because I for one know I'd never find another man like you in the whole wide world.'

'You're drunk.'

'After three glasses of wine? You underestimate me!'

'The only thing I underestimate is your ability to count how many glasses of wine you have actually drunk. Are you going to tell me something about this college chum of yours?'

'We met. He asked me how I was.'

'You didn't ask him?'

'Yes.'

'So what's he doing?'

'What do you mean, what's he doing? He's got a wife and two children. And he works in television. If that's what you mean.'

'Did you go and find somewhere to sit?'

'You didn't expect us to stand on the corner in that heat, did you?'

'And he wasn't with you today?'

'Today I was with Olga.'

'So you say.'

'Are you saying I'm lying?'

'I didn't say anything of the sort.'

'No, you only hinted at it. You just don't believe me. You should give your assistant a good ticking-off for failing to follow me closely enough. Or maybe hire an agency. It's possible these days. You pay them and they can snoop out who I was sitting in the wine bar with. You're disgusting!'

'So I'm disgusting, am I? You come home at night drunk and I'm the disgusting one.'

'I didn't come home at night and I'm more sober after a bottle of wine than you are after two glasses of lemonade.'

'Who's the dark-haired guy? Surely you can say a couple of normal sentences to me?'

'He's a fellow student from Kolín. We bumped into each other at the bottom of Wenceslas Square. I had an hour free and we went and sat somewhere. What interests you is if we made a date. No, we didn't. But he gave me his telephone number. Do you want it?'

'No, but I'm getting tired of your evasions.'

'I'm the one doing the evading? I toil for hours at school and then rush home here in a sweat in order to look after you lot. Then, out of the kindness of your heart, you offer me a week off and after five days you interrogate me as if I was your slave.'

'You're far from being a slave, very far. But you still haven't answered me.'

'And I don't intend to, because I find both your tone and this whole interrogation insulting.'

'Okay. Well, I find the situation you're placing me in degrading.'

'I'm placing you in some kind of situation?'

'Yes. Even my assistant has already . . .'

'God in heaven, why do I have to keep hearing about that fool?'

'It's me who's the fool, not him, for putting up with this.'

'So don't put up with it then. Just leave me alone.'

'What's that supposed to mean, "don't put up with it"?'

'Seeing as I don't know what you actually object to, I can't tell what it implies. What I do know is that you've spoiled my mood, and that I don't want to listen to you any more.'

'Now or ever again?'

'Now and preferably never again.'

'Fine. We can get a divorce.'

'Okay, then.'

'You can say it just like that?'

'It was you who said it, not me.'

'I said it because I know that's all you're waiting for.'

'Maybe it is, but it's you who said it. And besides, you'll never divorce me because you know full well you'd never find anyone else to put up with you, not even if you sent all your assistants out scouting.'

(1994)

About Love and Death

URANUS IN THE HOUSE OF DEATH

Only very rarely is someone from Prague invited to Australia with their fare and expenses paid. Director Michal Vrba received an invitation to a theatre festival due to take place in the city of Adelaide during March. The festival was linked to all sorts of exhibitions, conferences and debates. To judge from the programme enclosed with the invitation, the distant seaport with the sweet maidenly name would be sagging under the weight of cultural events during the festival.

Michal tended to be a doer who regarded talk about theatre as a waste of time, since everything that could be said about theatre had already been written long ago. None the less the invitation pleased him – thrilled him in fact. He replied immediately, saying that he accepted the invitation to speak about Czech theatre and was looking forward to visiting the antipodes.

Regarding himself as a free agent (he had been divorced several years earlier) he could see nothing to prevent him taking the trip.

When he arrived that evening at Leona's (Leona's real name

was Alena, but from the moment she became his lover he had called her Leona; it sounded more arty) he told her about his trip with almost excessive enthusiasm. He exaggerated because he was unsure how she would react to the news and he wanted to make it clear that he was going whether she liked it or not.

'And they didn't invite me?' she wanted to know.

'I don't think they even invited wives.'

Leona acted in the small theatre where he was the sole director, as well as administrator, manager, and, most of the time, author of the plays (or rather poetical compilations.) He had trained as an economist, however, and defected to the theatre because economics bored him. But his knowledge came in handy as he had some inkling at least about market forces. He found Leona attractive – she was tall and slender with small breasts and a soft voice – and she was alluringly eccentric. Whenever she got drunk, which was quite often, she wanted to make love to him, no matter where they happened to be. Then she would demand, 'What have you done to me?' And she would expect him to reply in the most direct terms. Apart from that she was interested in all sorts of magic. She made regular visits to an astrologer and consulted fortune-tellers and homoeopaths. Michal didn't believe in any of that stuff, but so long as she brought him indisputable predictions about the good prospects of their relationship, or possible dangers for their theatre, or potential economic opportunities, he accepted it as part of their amatory conversations. He had therefore already provided her with the precise details about the moment when he left his mother's womb, and from time to time even allowed her to tell his fortune from the cards, which almost always foretold love and stressed with surprising frequency his artistic proclivities.

'Last time my tarot-reader talked about a long journey,' she now recalled. 'I thought she was talking about me, but now I see she meant both of us.'

She obviously regarded the fact that the journey was foretold as a good omen, or, more accurately, it meant that she could not receive the news other than as confirmation of what was intended to happen. That eased his mind and he started to wonder whether, since he had the rare chance of travelling such a long way, he shouldn't stay there for at least a month. That idea didn't appeal to Leona. What was she supposed to do here while he was off globe-trotting?

'When I come back we'll take a lovely holiday together,' he promised.

'Yes, we'll take a bus ride into the country. That'll be a great holiday. But go where you like, I'm sure I'll find something to do here while you're away.' It sounded like a threat, but he pretended not to have heard, as he disliked quarrels.

Then he returned to his usual routine: rehearsals, performances and scrounging for money, but in addition he had to spend the evenings writing his paper for the conference. He decided to write about small theatres, not simply because they were the ones he was most familiar with, but also because he was convinced that they were the only thing it was possible to say anything interesting about, since only they, if the theatre was going to survive, had any future. The theatre, he maintained, was one of the last places where the spectator could still personally witness the act of creation. However, the big theatres so alienated the audience from the actor, that instead of witnessing the act of creation they could only witness its effect. For a public brought up on television, the theatrical stage was no more than a big TV screen, the only thing special about it being its three-dimensionality, and technical advances were bound to rob it of that remaining uniqueness before long. By contrast, small theatres facilitated mutual contact. The act of creation had far-reaching implications in today's hypertech world. It had become the only way for the human spirit to escape both the stultifying stereotype of the mundane and the depths towards which it is drawn by the dark forces of that banality that encourages and accumulates within it.

He visited Leona almost every day. During supper about a week before his departure, when he was in the grip of pre-travel nerves, Leona suddenly said to him:

'You mustn't fly there.'

'Fly where?' he gasped.

'You mustn't fly anywhere. You should be extremely cautious about what you do because you have Uranus in your eighth house.'

'So?'

'It's the house of death!'

'How did you figure that out?'

'I went to see my astrologer. After all, I have to consult him when you're planning a journey like that!'

'You know I don't believe in it.' Astrology happened to be one of the dark forces that enticed people into the depths.

'It's immaterial whether you believe it or not. What must happen will happen.'

'And what must happen?'

'Michal,' she said, 'this journey of yours won't turn out well. Apart from that, your Saturn is in opposition to Uranus. My astrologer told me he'd never seen such a depressing constellation.'

'Are you trying to tell me my plane is going to crash?'

'I've no idea what will happen. All I know is that your journey can't turn out well for you.'

'Who has worked this out, you or your ridiculous astrologer?'

'He's not ridiculous. He's one of the best astrologers there is. Everyone says so.'

'Everyone who believes that nonsense.'

'I believe him. Everything he foresaw for me came true.'

'For instance.'

'He foresaw you.'

'He foresaw me?'

'Yes, he told me I'd meet you.'

'That you'd meet me and not just some guy?'

'That I'd meet you.'

'Did he tell you my name?'

She hesitated. 'He said I'd meet a Virgo with strong artistic leanings, and that it would turn out well for me.'

Admittedly the 'strong artistic leanings' flattered him but he had no intention of changing his views about superstitions. 'I don't believe in it. It's quite simple, you do and I don't!'

'So you're determined to fly in spite of the warning?'

'Of course. I've already got my ticket.'

'But something's going to happen to you, for God's sake!'

'Forget about it.'

Then they made love as usual. When he woke up in the night he noticed she was sitting on the bed looking at him. 'What's up?'

'I'm looking at you.' Then she put her arms around him. 'Darling, you mustn't go, you really mustn't. Something will happen to you. Something terrible!' And she burst into tears.

Then they sat together on the divan until morning while he

tried to explain to her that there was either no connection at all between the position of the planets in the heavens and the fate of people on earth, or that it was so insignificant it was outweighed by thousands of other, more important considerations. Besides – it occurred to him – if the position of the planets really was crucial, then all those people born at the same moment would have to have virtually the same fate. And that was clearly nonsense. Or was she trying to tell him that everyone boarding that aircraft had Uranus in their house of death?

She told him she wasn't saying anything about the plane, only about him.

But if some calamity was awaiting him, he would be just as likely to encounter it here as in the antipodes.

No, she was here to protect him. Besides, the astrologer had told her he definitely shouldn't fly.

It struck Michal that Leona simply didn't want to let him go, that she was jealous of his trip and it so incensed him he started to shout at her.

She started to weep hysterically. The way actresses know how to.

At that afternoon's rehearsal (they were preparing a programme of Tibetan poetry), she had recited the verses: *You can tell wise men from fools because they see things that have not yet come, although come they surely must.* She said the words with such emphasis that there could be no doubting who the message was intended for. Most likely all the company already knew that Uranus resided in his house of death and that in spite of it he was determined to fly to his doom. He certainly had the impression that they were looking at him as if seeing him alive for the last time.

He had to change in London to catch the Australian airline's plane. When he first caught sight of the enormous jumbo jet through the glass of the terminal (he had never even set eyes before on such a colossus, let alone flown in one), it struck him as unbelievable that such a gigantic heap of metal could fly at all. And if it did (as it undoubtedly could) then it must be particularly vulnerable. This thought about its vulnerability naturally had nothing to do with any ridiculous astrological superstitions, it was something that must inevitably strike anyone boarding a transoceanic plane of that size. Even so it was statistically proven that air travel is by far the safest form of transport, and since tens of millions of passengers travelled that way every year, a good few thousand of them were bound to have Uranus or some other planet in their house of death. Although it was also a fact that planes did crash from time to time – due to some technical fault, of course, not because some of the passengers had Uranus or Saturn . . . He decided he would quite simply stop thinking about Uranus in his death house and joined the queue of those waiting to expose their luggage and themselves to the all-seeing rays. He noticed that the man in front of him had his hat pulled down low over his eyes and that he had dark glasses and a broad criminal chin. He looked just like a screen or stage gangster (Michal must have encountered real live gangsters on many occasions in the past, but their criminal nature had remained hidden from him). When the man placed his bag on the conveyor belt, the uniformed attendant seated at the screen happened to be looking away and exchanging a few words with a passing air hostess. Had there been a bomb hidden in the bag it would have gone undetected. Anyway, as far as he knew, X-rays weren't able to detect Semtex. There was nothing for it but to put his faith in

Providence and trust blindly that the 350 or so passengers did not include even one suicidal maniac.

What percentage of the world's population was suicidal maniacs? And the percentage of ordinary suicidal individuals? If someone is intent on killing himself why shouldn't he take along a few dozen others who would prefer to survive?

As he was leaving, Leona gave him a letter, asking him to open it before he boarded the plane. He had been determined not to open it until he was in the plane, but because he was obliged to wait in the terminal building he pulled the envelope out of his pocket and opened it.

My one and only darling,
Don't get on the plane. Don't fly anywhere. Australia is a country like any other. You can see kangaroos at the zoo and you wouldn't learn anything about the theatre even if you did arrive. But I'm afraid you won't. I know you won't. I want you. I need you alive.

The call for the first batch of passengers came over the PA. He folded up the letter, which he actually found quite touching, and put it back in his pocket. For a moment he toyed with the idea of not boarding. He'd simply announce that he was not going aboard because he was afraid.

Afraid of what?

He had received a serious warning. However, it concerned only him.

Fine, that's your business. But your tickets will no longer be valid.

Tickets, tickets, what did tickets matter compared to his own life?

He would still be sitting here in the terminal when the first news of the tragic accident came on the television. They would put his survival down to miraculous good fortune. He could actually visualize the headlines, *Another Triumph for Astrology!* And how would he get home? Or was he going to stay sitting here in the terminal until Uranus slipped out of his house of death? Meanwhile the festival would be over and he would never get a chance to cross the equator, see the Southern Cross or set his face to the cold southern breeze bringing with it the scent of the Antarctic.

Now they were calling his row, so he stood up and joined the crowd swarming onto the plane.

He did not catch sight of the gangster on board, but that did not reassure him. In fact it had the opposite effect. The aircraft was a double-decker so he hadn't the faintest idea who was on the lower floor.

On one side of him sat a man with protruding ears and a Mafia-style moustache who greeted him with a 'Buona sera' and then mumbled something unintelligible. On the other side, there was quite an interesting-looking blonde who immediately started reading an English-language booklet.

He had also brought some books with him but instead he took the letter out of his pocket. He was moved by the fact that Leona was so afraid for him. As soon as he stepped off the plane onto Australian soil he would call her. Assuming he ever found himself on Australian soil.

The aircraft slowly and quietly started to move. Its enormous bulk rolled along the concrete runway. A map flashed onto the television screen in front of him with the route of the flight. Height zero, speed 1 knot.

Then the aircraft came to a halt and the jet engines suddenly roared into life. The stewardess was demonstrating how to attach the safety belt and how to put on the oxygen mask and lifebelt.

Did any of the stewardesses have their stars read before a flight? What would happen to a stewardess who refused to go on duty because she discovered Uranus was entering her house of death?

He took his notebook and pencil out of his pocket and started to write.

Sweetheart,
We've just taken off. The flight takes about sixteen hours with a stopover in Singapore. I'll send you a postcard from Singapore. Just so you know I was there and was thinking of you. If I don't write it will mean I didn't arrive as you prophesied but that I crashed thinking of you.

He suddenly realized that if he didn't arrive this piece of paper would never reach his lover, so he stuffed his notebook back in his pocket.

The stewardesses started bringing round drinks. Many stewardesses, many drinks. They also handed out headphones to listen to any of five radio programmes or the soundtrack for the films.

The blonde at his side closed her book, put on her headphones and listened intently to something for a while. Two little Indian girls chased each other up and down the aisle between the seats. Figures flashed onto the screen with the map. They were 400 kilometres from London at a height of 10,580 metres. Outside the window it was 47 degrees below zero.

He shut his eyes. He felt extremely lonely in this over-crowded space.

He didn't tend to think about death, but of all deaths the most horrible to his mind was death by drowning. One lacked nothing, one just needed to breathe and instead there was '*water, water everywhere*'.

In the middle of the ocean in a life jacket. As if anyone could ever free themselves from this enormous structure if it crashed into the sea. It suddenly struck him that the entire trip was pointless. He had no need to fly to Australia. It was gratu-itous pride, the pride of the modern man, who doesn't even know the neighbours in his block of flats yet can boast he has been to the antipodes. How many of the people here really needed to travel from one end of the world to the other? Pride comes before a fall. People invented that saying before they had any inkling that they would proudly fly and also fall.

It was interesting how many famous and presumably other-wise sensible people believed in astrology.

Australia – Austrology.

People wanted to believe in something, naturally. The thought of our journeys being unpredictable, solely dependent on chance circumstances, was too disheartening. Just like the thought that we came from nothing and would disappear into nothing.

The weakest return to nothingness was via water. When the water-logged lungs could no longer take in a single gasp of air. *Water, water everywhere.*

He wiped the sweat from his forehead.

The Mafioso at his side was muttering something under his breath. He was praying most likely. It struck him that everyone in this particular space was acting as if everything was all right when in fact they were gripped by fear. He could feel it; the atoms of panic were floating in the air: silent, sticky and oppressive.

The fair-haired woman at his side took off her headphones and turned to ask him where he was flying to. As if he could fly anywhere else apart from the plane's destination.

But she was flying on to New Zealand. She was a physics teacher from Dunedin.

No, he'd never been there.

Almost no one had been there apart from those who were born there or who had emigrated there. But it was a beautiful place at the southern tip of South Island. A rugged coastline, picturesque with cliffs, seals and cormorants.

It struck him that as a physics teacher she was bound to know something about the laws which allowed such a colossus to hold itself up at this frosty height. She would also know something about the planets, and even astrology. But he was too shy to ask.

Food was brought round. They were already 1,080 kilometres from London and nearing the coast of Africa. But the surrounding air temperature had dropped another three degrees. The aircraft was travelling at a speed of 970 kilometres per hour.

He finished his meal. The stewardesses gave out lightweight slippers, pillows, blankets and black eye-masks.

He had hardly slept a wink the night before his departure. First he had taken leave of his friends and then of Leona. She hadn't tried to dissuade him any more but had simply given him the letter as they parted. He suppressed the urge to read the dismal prophecy once more. No, it would be pointless by now. He ought to sleep instead. Or at least think about something cheerful, such as the antipodean theatre festival, a land full of strange plants and animals, or a sky full of stars that he had never set eyes on before.

He tipped his seat back, placed a pillow under his head and covered his eyes with the black band.

All of a sudden he realized that within that constantly roaring blend of noises he could make out the regular ticking – albeit very quiet – of some kind of clock.

A time bomb. Somewhere right under his seat. He had an urge to leap up and call over a stewardess straight away. But instead he slowly raised himself and leaned far enough over to look under the seat. To all appearances a neatly packed life jacket was stowed there. And anyway the ticking had stopped. He sat up. Scarcely was he upright than the ticking resumed. It seemed to come from the side where the blonde teacher from Dunedin was sitting. She was still reading.

Maybe he was raving.

Even so he plucked up courage and asked her if she could hear the ticking too.

Of course. She took a small alarm clock out of her handbag. She always took it with her because sometimes she needed to get up particularly early. But he certainly had extremely sharp ears to have noticed the ticking amidst all that din.

The Italian at his side was still muttering something. Behind him a child was crying. On the map spread out beneath them the coastline of a continent was visible. How many miles were there still to go? How many hours of uncertainty? But when, where and how could one find certainty? He shut his eyes.

Uranus in his house of death. Such nonsense. *My one and only darling, I'm afraid you won't arrive. I know you won't.*

He screwed up his courage once more and asked his neighbour whether she was interested in astrology?

Of course, she replied and smiled delightedly. It's my hobby. I know how to draw up horoscopes, both radical and progressive charts. I have a whole bundle of star charts at home. Our fates are predetermined, you know. Our only problem is not knowing how to read them properly yet.

Do you really think so? Sorry, I'm Michal.

I'm Jane. Yes, I really do. I know so.

May I ask you something, Jane?

Of course, ask away, Michal, ask away, darling.

In which house is your Uranus, Jane?

In the house of death. And yours?

Mine is too, Jane. So how come you risked taking this flight?

Because there's no escaping your fate. Only foolish people think they will manage to. The foolish are always on the run. Or on the attack. Or building towers. They think they are building towers when in point of fact they are building labyrinths in which they will die anyway.

You're not afraid of dying?

Why should I be, seeing that we are going to die together? But darling, this is me, didn't you recognize me? I disguised myself so I could be with you. Far better to end it for good in the ocean waves than spend a holiday just outside Prague. Your house of death will be mine too!

Leona!

At that moment a deafening explosion shot him into the air and then there began a long, terrifying final descent into the depths. He saw the rapidly approaching surface of the water and in paralysing terror he opened his eyes. The young woman alongside him was asleep. The lights in the plane were dimmed. On the screen in front of him the dark spot of the aircraft moved across the Indian Ocean.

When at last he disembarked at Sydney airport and found out how many dollars a three-minute phone call to Prague cost, he decided to call Leona. He announced triumphantly that he had landed in the antipodes in spite of her astrologer's forecast.

'I know you landed safely,' she said.

'You know?' he marvelled. 'But you prophesied . . .'

'I miscalculated,' she quickly interrupted him. 'I was counting September as the tenth month, when in fact it's the ninth, of course. I gave my astrologer faulty information. I only realized my mistake after you'd taken off. You're a Virgo, of course, not a Libra. I don't know how I could have made that mistake. Your Uranus wasn't in the house of death, but in the house of love instead.'

'I don't believe this. Just imagine what would have happened if I'd let myself be dissuaded and stayed at home!'

'What would have happened? You'd be with me,' she said. 'You ought to be with me now anyway, seeing you've got Uranus in your house of love.'

(1994)

IT'S RAINING OUT

It was true that Judge Martin Vacek had dealt with a number of political cases under the old regime, but as he was only five years off retirement age, it was suggested to him that from now on he should deal exclusively with divorce cases (which, anyway, is what he used to do when he first came to the bench). He considered this to be an acceptable, even sensible proposal. He could, of course, have left the bench altogether, as several of his colleagues had done, and set up privately as a barrister, which was far more lucrative. But he was conservative by nature and had no wish to alter his daily routine and his regular journey to work, let alone have to start looking for and equipping private chambers. None the less, he consulted his wife about what he should do.

He had been married for thirty years and had stopped loving his wife Marie long ago; in fact he could no longer remember a time when he did actually love her. Nevertheless they got on fairly well together and he had been accustomed to consult her about career decisions, and even about some of the more complicated cases he had to try. His wife, who was a year older, came from the country and had no more than elementary schooling; she had spent her life working at the post office for paltry wages. She did, however, have a natural wisdom, which was fortunately unspoilt by a legal training. Marie had plainly stopped loving him years ago too, but she looked after him almost like a mother, cooking him good meals and making sure not only that his shirts were ironed but also that he had a suitable tie to wear with them. In the course of their life together she was bound to have influenced if not his character then at least his appearance, and since they both favoured the colour grey, their very features gradually began to take on a grey hue too. In recent years they had come to regard each other as an indispensable part of the household, particularly now that their two sons had grown up and moved away and the apartment felt empty, although crammed with all sorts of essentially useless objects and knick-knacks. They barely spoke any more, although there was a time when they used to go out together to the cinema or a concert (it was the done thing for someone in his position to have a season ticket for the philharmonic concerts), or Marie would relate to him the plots of novels she had read as he didn't have the time to. Nowadays, though, they didn't go to the cinema and simply exchanged a few words about food, shopping, their sons or the weather, or they simply watched the television together in silence. Marie no longer told him anything about what she read, if she read anything at all these days. It therefore came as a surprise to her when he asked her whether he should remain on the bench or start something completely fresh. It was not her custom to contradict her husband and when in the past he had asked her opinion on something, she had always tried to guess the reply he was wanting to hear. 'Divorce suits –' she now said, '– that could be fairly interesting work. You'll get to hear lots of stories.'

It had never occurred to him to view his possible future employment from such an angle. He had heard so many stories in his lifetime that they had long since ceased to interest him. None the less he took his wife's opinion into account and remained on the bench.

As it turned out, the cases tended to be more banal than interesting. In most of them, immature men had married young women who yearned for something that their husbands could not provide, so in time there appeared a third person who disrupted what had never been firmly established in the first place. Even so, his summing up was often met with tears. He would divorce couples on grounds of infidelity or mutual incompatibility. Some of them were husbands and wives who had stopped living together long ago, but in spite of that, he could never rid himself of the conviction that most of the divorces were unnecessary, that people were attempting to escape the inescapable: their own emptiness, their own incapacity to share their lives with another person. At least to the extent he had managed to himself.

There were so many cases that they soon became indistinguishable and even the people's faces slipped quickly from his memory – which was beginning to decline with age anyway. Now and then, however, a more interesting case would crop up, and a face, a name or an occupation would stick in his mind.

After one such a sitting, he emerged from the courtroom to discover the woman he had just divorced sitting opposite him on a bench in the corridor, crying.

The woman's name was Lída Vachková, a name that had immediately caught his eye because of its resemblance to his own, quite apart from the fact that the woman's distinctive, delicate beauty and her timid replies to his questions had held his attention in court. He attributed her delicacy to her profession; she was a violinist. Although it was uncharacteristic of him, he stopped in front of her and said, 'Don't cry, Mrs Vachková, no pain lasts for ever.'

She glanced up at him in surprise and quickly wiped away her tears. 'Thank you.' As she got up she started to sway and he was obliged to catch hold of her. 'Are you feeling unwell?'

'Do forgive me,' she said, 'I took some tablets this morning. To calm my nerves.'

He invited her into his chambers and fetched her a glass of water. He knew not only her name and occupation but also her age. She was twenty years his junior, very young, in his eyes, at least. He also knew the man who until a short while ago had been her husband. He too was older than she was (although at this moment he couldn't exactly recall how much older) and ran some recently established entertainment agency. A vulgar, unpleasant-looking fellow, he had apparently subjected his wife to rough and domineering treatment and had sought to curb all her interests. There were no children. They had had no problem agreeing on the division of their property – there wasn't very much anyway. The man had left the flat to his wife and moved in with his mistress.

'Do you really believe no pain lasts for ever?' she asked.

'Of course.'

'Did you ever have a pain that went away in the end?'

He was not accustomed to being cross-examined and was taken unawares. He had to stop and think for a moment whether anything had happened in his life that had caused him a pain that had gone away. On the contrary, things in his life had tended to die gradually. Then he recalled the death of his parents. 'Even the pain of death eventually goes away,' he said evasively.

'That's true,' she conceded, 'though death is a rather special category.'

'What makes you think so?'

'Death is like the law. There is no escape from it. Whereas love . . .' She seemed to be searching for a word to express the meaning of love, but instead burst into tears once again.

He helped her to her feet and saw her to the door and down the stairs. He then invited her to a nearby wine bar. He wasn't sure why, with this young woman, he was behaving in this way. There must be something about her that touched him, or that he found attractive. Or maybe there was some other reason that he was unable to put his finger on. He ordered a bottle of wine and let the woman relate her recent tribulations, although he only took in a few details; he was gazing at her hands, her fingers involuntarily toying with the napkin. They were so beautiful he wanted to clasp them or stroke them. So from time to time he would interrupt her and tell her some of the incidents he had heard about in the course of his work to reassure her that she was far from alone in her suffering.

When they parted an hour later, she invited him to a concert to be performed by the orchestra she played in. She also, naturally, invited his wife, but in the end he went to it alone. He found it impossible to concentrate on the music; his attention was focused on a single member of the orchestra – the flickering movements of her fingers and her fine bowing – and he felt an unwonted emotion. He was astounded at himself and at his feelings, which struck him as inappropriate for someone of his age. But then it occurred to him that he had simply written off feelings from his life too soon.

He found her address and telephone number in the file.

They started to meet twice a week, initially in a café or a wine bar, fairly typically. He was aware that because of his profession she regarded him as an expert on matters of love, or rather on those cases where love was foundering, and indeed when questioned he sought to draw more general lessons from the cases that lay hidden in his memory. Even though he had little belief in the possibility of people living together in love, he realized how cautious he was in his comments, and how he could speak about something he had been unable to achieve in his own life: a relationship of mutual admiration and respect out of which tenderness grew. She listened to him with interest and even a sort of growing hopefulness. 'I expect you're good at love,' she said and gave his hand a momentary squeeze. 'You strike me as someone who can be tolerant and allow the other person some space for themselves.'

He nodded, pleased that she should think of him in that way.

Then she invited him home.

She lived in a tiny attic room and as he walked up the many stairs (the house had no lift) his legs were buckling under him from excitement or maybe anxiety at what was certainly about to happen.

The little room had sloping walls and almost no furniture, just a wardrobe, a music stand, two chairs and a large divan beneath a skylight. They made love underneath that window.

She seemed slim and finely built compared to his wife and her skin was smooth, without a single fold or wrinkle. To his surprise, he found tender words for her. She listened to him and he had barely stopped speaking when she said, 'More please. I want more of those words.' As he was leaving she asked, 'Will we see each other again some time?' And he assured her that he would certainly be back soon.

And so he would visit her, bringing her flowers, wine and words of tenderness. They never spoke about her former marriage, and he mentioned his wife only occasionally, and always in a way that let her assume that his marriage was not particularly happy. As usually happens when information comes from one side only, she would conclude, had she made the effort, that the fault lay with his wife.

On one occasion, when they were again lying beneath the skylight onto which the heavy drops of a spring downpour were falling, she asked him, 'Do you love your wife at all?'

He said he didn't, that he hadn't loved her for many years.

Then for a long time neither of them said anything. She cuddled up to him as he stroked her flanks and her belly, the softness of her skin exciting him as always.

'What's the point of such a marriage, Martin?' she asked abruptly.

The question caught him unprepared. It had never occurred to him that he might leave his wife after thirty years of living together, not even now, as he lay at the side of a woman he had just made love to. He had long ceased wondering what bound him to his wife Marie. Habit perhaps. So many shared days and nights. Memories that now felt like stories about someone else. Maybe the chairs they sat on, or the familiar odour that wafted towards him the moment he opened the door of their flat. Maybe the sons they had reared.

'You don't have to tell me if you don't want to,' she said.

'Maybe,' it occurred to him, 'so that when I come home in foul weather like this I can say to someone, "It's raining out".'

'Yes, that's a good reason,' she said, drawing away from him slightly.

As he was leaving she didn't ask, as she usually did, when they would see each other again. So he asked instead.

'Maybe never,' she said. Even so she leaned towards him and kissed him.

On his way downstairs it occurred him that she had been expecting a different response, that he had mistaken the meaning of her question. She had been wanting to hear whether he was prepared to leave his wife for her.

He was overcome by an almost weary dejection. He could still turn back, ring her doorbell and give her a different answer. But what answer should he give?

So Judge Martin Vacek went on home.

When he opened the door of his own flat the familiar odour wafted towards him. Marie came out of the living room and greeted him as usual with the words: 'I'll have your dinner ready straight away.'

He sat down at the table and stared silently ahead of him. He saw nothing. On the radio which his wife had switched on in the adjoining room someone was playing the violin. He found the sound of it so distressing he could hardly move. His wife placed a bowl of hot soup in front of him.

He knew he ought to say something, but he was filled with an emptiness that engulfed all speech. 'It's raining out,' he said eventually.

His wife looked out of the window in surprise. It had stopped raining long ago and the room was suffused with the dark red glow of the setting sun.

It was her custom not to contradict her husband, even though he had seemed to her more and more absent-minded just lately; perhaps old age was beginning to affect his mind.

'That's good,' she said, 'the farmers' fields could do with a bit of moisture.'

(1994)

A BAFFLING CHOICE

Marie Anna Pavlů was almost twenty-six years old and worked as a nurse in a crèche. There was nothing striking about her appearance or behaviour. She had a pleasant face, a petite figure and a slight, almost deferential, stoop. She used no make-up and dressed simply, choosing darker shades of green and blue. Her most colourful feature was her hair which had a coppery sheen in the sun. Her expression was enlivened with a smile, particularly when dealing with children. The more attentive parents noticed that children tended to cry less when Marie welcomed them.

She had scarcely reached adulthood when she married Jakub Pavlů, a programmer. They had met at college. He was a good dancer and enjoyed company but drank moderately. He used to sing when he was in the mood – he had an enormous repertoire, as if he had an add-on memory in his head. Before they were married they used to leave every Friday afternoon with a group of his friends and go to a weekend chalet site. The little chalets were huddled together so closely that every word from the neighbouring cabin – every breath – was clearly audible. When she and Jakub made love there – it was the only place they could make love at the time – she uttered no sound at all. He assumed that she was shy because of the lack of privacy: it didn't occur to him that she was not aroused by him. Subsequently, when they were already living together, her mute passivity might have become more noticeable, but by then he was used to it and accepted the fact that his wife was timid and reserved by nature. Besides, he was not one of those men who think about giving their partner sexual pleasure.

A son was born two years after their wedding and they named him Matouš. He was a quiet baby who seldom cried, and when Marie spoke to him he seemed to understand what she was saying but was simply unable to reply. However, he did start to speak earlier than little boys usually do. Before he was even three Marie became accustomed to chatting to him as if they were the same age. It seemed to her that he was capable of sensing her mood, so that he would laugh if she was feeling fine and try to humour her when she was miserable. Then he suddenly fell ill with thymic asthma and almost suffocated to death with the first unexpected fit of coughing.

From that moment Marie lived in fear of another bout returning and killing her little boy while she was asleep. She would often leap out of bed at night and run to listen to his breathing. Afterwards she would find herself weeping inexplicably. She was simply aware of a vague sorrow that life should contain so much alienation, suffering and death. She felt sorry for other people's children who were brought to her every morning half asleep and crying, and for her own Matouš, whom she too delivered up to strangers even though she knew he would prefer to stay with her.

She herself had had little contact with her parents as a child. Her mother, a bad reporter on a bad newspaper, was away on assignments most of the time. Her father was a drunkard and a gambler who moved out shortly after Marie was born. She only saw him a few times a year. She was mostly in the care of her maternal grandmother, who also lived alone, but remarried when Marie was ten years old. Although in his sixties, her grandmother's new husband was still a vigorous man. He was rather boisterous and talked a lot. He also spoke more loudly than other people, so that at first Marie was scared of him. He had barely moved in before he was decorating the living room – her favourite place – to suit himself. He unpacked books from tea chests and decked the walls with glass cases of moths, landscapes in oils by Romantic masters and several antique puppets. The room no longer looked like the one she had been used to. Whenever she was in it she was overcome with a feeling of dejection and slight dread as if in anticipation of some unwelcome surprise.

Her step-grandfather soon became fond of her and actually seemed to brighten up in her presence. He enjoyed chatting with her and wanted to hear all her news each day. He gave her the impression he was genuinely interested in her prattle. Back in what was for her the inconceivably distant past, he had been a teacher of natural history. He had taught for only a short time – three years after the war they had sacked him on the grounds of political unreliability. Since then, he had earned his living in all sorts of jobs – ending up as a museum attendant. 'I started with natural history collections and ended with them!' And he would laugh as if fate had played a clever trick on him. Everything he said seemed to turn into a succession of weird or funny stories and encounters, or homilies and words of wisdom. Often she wouldn't understand them, but there were sentences or images that stayed in her memory. Sometimes when they went for walks together he would sniff with delight scents she had hardly noticed and point out to her the natural markings in a stone she had been oblivious to. He would encourage her to listen to the scarcely audible sounds of the forest, and at dusk would make her look up at the sky. 'Stargazing raises the spirits and brings relief at moments of trouble, because it puts everything – all your joys, quarrels and heartache – into proper perspective.' He would impress on her that one must never despair whatever happens, because life gives everyone a chance to make their mark through some deed or other – to shine, to rise above the seeming futility of human existence. The opportunity might come at any moment, and often it was unremarkable because it could easily involve something small rather than something large. It might be to do with the life of a woman, or the life of a tree; it might mean relieving the suffering of a person, or a bird, or of the water, or the air.

When she was fifteen, her grandfather suffered a stroke that left his legs paralysed. He would move around the flat on crutches but refused to let her help him. He used to sit in the big wing chair and tell her stories in a faltering voice. A few weeks later he suffered another stroke and lost the power of speech entirely. When she came to visit him in hospital he definitely recognized her, but his mouth was no longer capable of smiling. She leaned over and kissed him and then burst into tears. How much suffering the departure from this life can entail which no one else can relieve, even when the one departing is the person you love best of all.

When she first met Jakub, her grandfather was already long

dead, but it struck her that the moment her grandfather had spoken of had finally arrived. Something would change in their lives to rid them of triviality and the pathetic striving after ephemera. But nothing of the sort happened.

It was several years before they moved into a flat of their own. It was on the seventh floor of a thirteen-storey panel-built block. The windows looked out onto equally unprepossessing concrete walls. In place of lawns, the areas in between the blocks of flats were filled with piles of earth, planks and stone. As it was only a few minutes' walk to the crèche where she worked, she spent her life amidst the half-finished housing estate. She tried to furnish the flat as simply as possible and made up for the lack of belongings with fresh flowers. She took proper care of her husband and her little boy even though it took up most of the time she might have had for herself. She cooked every day and baked home-made bread, buns or tarts for Sundays, the way women did in the old days.

Her husband just took it all for granted, and showed no sign of satisfaction or dissatisfaction. He was sparing with his affection not because he didn't love her, but because he was convinced that it was the husband's role to be reserved and condescending towards his wife.

For several years this was the pattern of their life together; for her it was quiet, monotonous and lonely. She knew none of the other tenants, even though they were mostly of her own age. Jeans and jean-jackets, trainers, tinted hair, the same deodorants and make-up, the same greetings said with the same intonation – everything and everyone became indistinguishable. Only in the flat below theirs lived an old man who was different from the others both in age and appearance: he walked with the aid of crutches.

On the odd occasion that they met by the lift in the hallway, she would hold the door open for him until he had manoeuvred himself in. As the lift went up, the old man would keep his gaze fixed on her. Several times she thought he was about to say something to her, but he apparently thought better of it or realized that he wouldn't manage to say all he wanted to by the time they reached his floor. Once she found him carrying a large box. When the lift stopped at the sixth floor, she helped him carry the parcel to the door of his flat. As soon as he opened his door, a mixture of organic and chemical smells wafted towards her. From inside the flat she could hear a parrot squawking and a fat tom-cat came and rubbed up against the old man's legs. The man started to thank her and she quickly said goodbye. As she was closing the door behind her she read his name on the door. It struck her that he must have been a very good-looking man in his youth. Everything about him was powerful, but most of all his hands, neck and chin. He still had a thick head of hair, even though it was nearly white. What had happened to him to make him need crutches? Then she stopped thinking about him.

The very next day she met him again in front of the flats as she was coming home from work. He greeted her and she smiled at him. She met him three more times that week – an odd coincidence, if it was a coincidence. On the third occasion, he was carrying a bunch of roses and as he was leaving the lift he handed them to her.

'But you can't have bought them for me!' she protested.

'Maybe I did,' he said and hobbled out of the lift.

The scent of the flowers filled her with a sense of vague expectation. When she put them into a vase she could not help smiling at her own feelings.

She baked some tarts for the weekend and set some aside, putting them in a chocolate box and then wrapping the box in tissue paper.

The old man lived in a single room that was more like a workshop or studio. Alongside a work bench stood a wooden press and a guillotine whose blade pointed upwards and made her feel queasy. Along the walls there were untidy heaps of books and papers. And the shelves and chairs were piled high with things too. The tom-cat was sleeping on the divan surrounded by a heap of discarded clothes. She noticed a number of unframed paintings – old-fashioned, romantic subjects that seemed out of keeping with the newness of the painting. Only then did she become aware of a painter's easel and on it a portrait in progress. She stared in consternation at the unfinished face. There could be no doubt: it was her own.

'I never studied painting,' she heard him say from behind her. He laid the box she had brought him on a table without opening it and hurriedly started to clear one of the chairs. 'I spent my whole life binding books. This is a new thing. I was attracted by the way you looked. You have so much noble beauty. Unfortunately I'm unable to capture it. There's something of our Slav forebears in you . . .' The chair was now empty but she did not sit down. She apologized for arriving unannounced and quickly left.

Back in her own flat she rushed to the mirror and gazed at herself for a moment before realizing that in reality her eyes were much smaller than in the painting. She tried to open them as wide as she could and smiled at her reflection.

The next day she picked up her son from kindergarten in the early afternoon as usual. Matouš talked incessantly. She usually enjoyed his mixture of childish notions, make-believe and actual experience but today she found she was unable to concentrate. When in the distance she caught sight of the old bookbinder waiting in front of the flats she took her son to the sandpit so that she could go into the building on her own. He greeted her and hobbled after her into the lift. 'I tidied the place up today,' he announced to her as soon as the lift started to move. 'Wouldn't you like to drop in for a minute or two?'

Her portrait was now covered with a clean sheet and the clutter had disappeared from the chairs and the divan.

After all there was nothing wrong in visiting an old invalid who was obviously lonely. She sat down by the window in order to keep an eye on the sandpit – and also to conceal her embarrassment. She refused his offer of refreshments.

The bookbinder laid his crutches aside and sat down with difficulty. For a moment he gazed at her mutely, but then started to ask her questions. Was she happy with her life? What sort of childhood had she had? Had she chosen her profession because she enjoyed being with children? It was his belief that people who looked after children fulfilled a noble mission.

His language was slightly overblown but what impressed her most was his interest in her life. A sudden sense of intimacy filled her with alarm and she swiftly made her excuses and hurried off to find her son.

She would call on the old bookbinder from time to time and bring him some cakes she had baked. For his part he would present her with either books or flowers. She read the books but they meant little to her as their subject matter was too far removed from her usual reading. She never stayed longer than a few minutes in the bookbinder's flat, but those short moments increasingly began to fill her thoughts.

She now knew everything about the bookbinder's life that he considered important for her to know. He was sixty-five. He had moved there from a village where his sister still lived. Originally he was to have taken over his father's farm, but in the last days of the war his leg had been blown off by a mine and he had almost bled to death. At the age of twenty he had felt that his life was at an end. In time, however, he had come to realize that there were doors still open to him, in spite of his misfortune. Doors to knowledge and mystical experience. All he had to do was muster the strength to break free of the external world with its passions and strivings and start to open the door to a higher bliss, to the vision of God. One door did remain closed. He could never start a family of his own. As the years went by, he gradually lost those close to him and he lived out his days in solitude, only visiting his sister during the summer. He was usually away at this time of year.

'Why are you still here, then?' she asked.

'But you know perfectly well why,' he replied.

It sometimes occurred to her that he made rather too much of the tranquillity and contentment he had achieved. She had the feeling that the equanimity on which he laid such stress merely concealed a deep longing as well as the wounds he had suffered in the distant past. At other times, she found his statements completely baffling. She could not understand his enthusiasm for the religion of the ancient Aryans and the mores of their Slav forebears, nor why he suspected the Jews of conspiring against all other nations. She didn't know any Jews anyway, let alone any Indians, and the concerns or practices of the ancient Slavs were alien to her. None the less she listened attentively to the old man as if wanting to make up for all the years when no one had listened to him.

At the end of spring, her husband was due to leave Prague for a week on business: whenever she thought of his departure she felt a thrill, though she wasn't quite sure why. The evening after Jakub's departure, she waited until her son was asleep and then changed into her best clothes. She sat down in front of the mirror and gazed at her face for a long time. She tried to apply some eyeshadow, but her hands trembled too much. Instead she went into the bedroom where her son was sleeping, kissed him on the forehead and then tiptoed out onto the landing. The noise of television sets was audible as she passed the other flats, but when she lightly pressed his doorbell it seemed as if the sound could be heard through all thirteen floors.

He came to the door. 'Is something wrong?'

She shook her head. She sat down on the chair, where she usually sat – on the occasions when she did sit. The bookbinder brought a bottle of wine and two glasses. 'Have you the time today?'

She noticed that there was a new picture of her on the wall but she was unable to concentrate on it.

'Has your husband gone?'

She nodded.

'A pity I'm so old,' he lamented, 'and a cripple into the bargain.'

'That's not important, is it? The main thing is I really enjoy being with you.' She was at a loss what to do. She stood up and turned towards the door, but stopped disconcerted in the middle of the room. 'Do you think I should go?'

'No, definitely not!'

She didn't look at him. Several dark cobwebs hung from the ceiling and the sound of music came through the wall.

The old man came over to her and kissed her on the neck. 'It's a long time since I have been with a woman. Many years.'

She put her arms around him. Suddenly all the embarrassment and uncertainty left her. She went over to the ottoman, took off her clothes and waited for him to join her.

He came and sat by her, gently calling her by the names of different Slav goddesses while stroking her forehead, her cheeks, her neck and her breasts. His words and his touch aroused a deep longing in her. She whispered words that came unexpectedly into her mind, as if she were weaving charms for herself and the old man. When at last he lay down beside her it was as if she had waited her whole life for this moment and she became aware of an unfamiliar delight that went on growing until she could bear it no longer and she let out a cry loud enough to penetrate all thirteen floors and rouse everyone, whether awake or asleep.

The bookbinder caressed her body with his coarse hands and waves of bliss washed over her again and again. 'I love you,' she whispered, 'I love you.' At that moment she overheard a strange barking sound coming from beyond the wall. Her son was suffocating.

She rushed out onto the landing half naked. When she opened the door she was greeted with total silence. She went numb at the thought of her son lying there lifeless, having choked to death while she wickedly indulged her passion.

But Matouš was asleep and breathing peacefully. One of his pillows had simply fallen off his bed onto the floor. 'Oh, my poor little lamb!' She knelt down and touched his forehead and the wisps of his hair that had grown damp as he slept. 'Mummy will never leave you on your own again!' She stretched out on the rug, put the child's pillow under her head and closed her eyes. Red spots danced before her eyes, swelling up and then dwindling again. Gradually butterflies' wings emerged and flittered above her, combining to form romantic landscapes. Then everything faded and went dark and out of the darkness emerged the figure of the old bookbinder. His face was bathed with light and, with a sudden sense of happiness, she realized that the light was coming from her.

The next evening, as soon as her son fell asleep she went to find the old man and spent most of the night with him. It was nearly morning when she returned. She lay down beside her son's bed and fell asleep straight away.

When Jakub returned a week later he found her haggard, as if exhausted from a fever. She avoided his kiss and was scarcely aware of what he was saying. Then she announced that she couldn't live with him any more and tried to explain to him what had happened. He listened to her aghast. When he had grasped the sordid nature of her infidelity, he yelled at her that she disgusted him. He was about to hit her but it seemed too theatrical and undignified, so he just spat on the floor and dashed out of the room. She could hear him shouting from the next room, most likely for her benefit but perhaps he wanted the person downstairs to hear. 'With a cripple like that – she goes and does it with a senile cripple!'

Marie put her son to bed. For a moment she hesitated over whether she should go to her husband and try and make him understand that she had no wish to hurt him. Then she realized that the old bookbinder was sure to be waiting for her and she crept out onto the landing.

When news of her behaviour spread, people were scandalized. Such a misalliance left all other adultery in the shade. A social worker voiced doubts about whether she was a suitable person to bring up her son and submitted a lengthy report to her superiors showing that the mother had left her child alone in the flat night after night. The director of the crèche asked her to find a job somewhere people didn't know her.

On the day of the divorce hearing, the old bookbinder accompanied her to court. He carefully stood his crutches against the wall and took a seat in the back row.

The judge was a stout, kindly looking man. In his time he had dissolved hundreds of marriages but he would always try to reconcile the couples, usually without success. He tried to reconcile Marie Anna with her husband too. Lots of unexpected things could happen in the course of a marriage, he told them. People found themselves in situations they would have never have dreamed of and so found it impossible to deal with them: at such moments they could take rash decisions that they would regret. It was up to their partners, if they loved them, to show forbearance and offer them a helping hand.

He turned to Marie and urged her to consider her actions and think not only about her partner who had so far behaved like a model husband, but also to take her son's interests into account. Nothing would ever make up for the comfort of a happy home. A child should be brought up by the joint efforts of both parents. Didn't she realize that she could lose her son not only by a court decision, but also by a judgement of the heart, were her son not to accept her actions when he was old enough to fully understand? And last but not least she should think about herself. After all, she too wanted to live with someone who was her equal, spend not just a few short months with him but live to see the fruits of their joint efforts, live with her partner to a ripe old age, when one needed the support of one's companion more than in one's youth. The judge looked towards the seats where her lover sat, whose early demise he seemed to prophesy, and then turned to her husband and asked him if he was still willing to take Marie back as his wife. Jakub seemed overcome with emotion and was about to say something when he simply nodded. The judge adjourned the hearing to give them time to think things over.

The three of them left the court room. Jakub hesitated for a moment, then, without a word, started to stride away, healthy and self-confident, while she walked along silently at the side of the lame old man.

The bookbinder talked continuously as if suddenly taken aback by his responsibility: the hearing was bound to have upset her and she must have been scared by the threat of her son being taken away from her by the authorities. It was an unlikely eventuality, but should there really be such a risk, she was not to take him, an old man, into account. He would leave and remove the burden that he was becoming to her.

She shook her head. In fact she hadn't found the hearing particularly upsetting. She felt that it had nothing to do with her and she had not yet absorbed the fact that she might lose her son.

The old man at her side picked up the judge's words about death and those who are left alone. He said he had no right to ask her to bind herself to him, to take her away from her family and then abandon her, leaving her alone in the world.

She listened to him horrified. How could he talk so cold-bloodedly if he loved her? How could he call into question the very thing that had raised them above what would otherwise be a meaningless existence?

She shook her head once more. Then they parted company and without another glance in his direction she hurried off to fetch her son. Only now did the judge's words begin to sink in. When Matouš ran up to meet her at the kindergarten, she took him in her arms, hugged him and burst into tears.

Back home she played with the little boy, then fed him and put him to bed. Her husband had gone off somewhere, but for the first time in ages she did not go down to the flat below.

In the bathroom she glanced in the mirror. She had grown thin over the past three weeks, her face struck her as emaciated, with her small eyes looking even more deeply set, surrounded by a dark shadow.

Jakub returned before midnight. His face showed momentary surprise but he walked past her in silence. He stank of beer.

She lay down in the bedroom which until recently she had shared with Jakub but which neither of them used these days. The judge had warned her about loneliness should she remain with the old man and he died before she did. As if death was governed solely by age, and death alone determined people's loneliness. As if a few months of love didn't mean more than a whole life without it.

She got up, put on her dressing gown, and quietly opened the door behind which her husband was lying. He wasn't asleep, he was smoking.

'Don't take him from me,' she said, meaning her son.

He didn't even turn his head towards her.

'I don't know why it happened,' she went on, 'but we were happy.'

Jakub made a gagging noise.

'Forgive me. I don't know why it happened.' She realized that he could never understand her choice and so he could hardly grant her this wish. Receiving no reply, she turned and left the room.

She stopped outside the door on the floor below but didn't ring the bell; she just stood and waited. She listened to the silence from inside. Nothing disturbed it. She realized she had no wish to disturb it either. A man may be a cripple, but he must remain a man who did not shy away from responsibility.

She walked down the remaining six floors.

Fate offered everyone a moment when they could shine, the chance of some deed to transcend their own emptiness. But when that moment passed, what then? What should follow?

She leaned wearily against the wall of the building. She looked upwards, but the light of the stars was obscured by the glow of the street lamps.

(1987)

RICH MEN TEND TO BE STRANGE

There are men who love women, there are men who love alcohol, nature or sport, there are men who love children or work, and there are men who love money. It is possible, of course, for a man to love more than one of these, but he will always give one priority over the rest. If he is sufficiently ambitious he can hope to achieve the thing he yearns for most.

Alois Burda loved money and subordinated everything else to it. Under the old regime he was the manager of a car mart, under the new one he opened one of his own. Under the old regime he had skilfully negotiated with the few cars he had for sale and soon found a way of maximizing bribes. After the revolution, his above-board commission gave him about the same income as he had enjoyed previously. Alois Burda was therefore a rich man and as early as the 1970s had built himself a family home with a living area (in accordance with the legislation then in force) of less than 120 square metres. In reality it was three times the size. The house contained a gymnasium, a covered swimming pool and three garages, and alongside it stood a tennis court, although he himself didn't play tennis. He had one secret bank account in Switzerland, and since the Swiss banks paid miserable interest rates, he had another in Germany. He had only been divorced once because he discovered that divorce could be a rather expensive business. With his first wife he had two sons, with his second, a daughter. He rarely saw his sons. Since they had grown up they didn't meet more than once a year. He soon grew tired of his second wife too, though she took fairly good care of the home and didn't bother him too much. Nor did she concern herself with how he spent his free time. She was fond of sports and went skiing and horse-riding, played tennis and golf and was a good swimmer, none of which interested him in the least. From time to time he would take a mistress, although he would seldom feel anything for her and expected nothing in return.

Occasionally he would ask his daughter for news from school, but he would forget her reply by the next morning and he was never entirely sure which class she was in. Then she too left school and got married. As a wedding present he gave her a new car that cost more than half a million crowns. The gift took her by surprise and she was almost ready to believe it was given with love, although it was more likely to salve his conscience or just a momentary whim. Besides, a sum like that meant nothing to Burda.

He knew a lot of people, since he had clients everywhere, but he had no real friends. At best he had a few cronies with whom he would go for a drink from time to time or dream up business deals.

As his sixtieth birthday approached, he suddenly started to suffer from exhaustion, lost his appetite and started losing weight. He put it down to his hectic lifestyle but his wife noticed the transformation in him and told him to go to the doctor. He ignored his wife's advice on principle, and was afraid the doctor would discover that there was something seriously wrong. He decided he would take things more easily and even take a non-business trip abroad. He also visited a well-known healer who mixed him a special herbal tea and recommended that he eat pumpkin seeds every day. But none of it did any good. Burda started to suffer from stomach pains and would wake up in the night soaked in perspiration, thirsty and in the grip of a strange anxiety.

Finally, he decided to see a doctor who was one of his oldest clients and had treated his first wife. The doctor tried to give the impression that everything was in order and chatted for a while about the latest Honda.

'Is it serious?' the car dealer asked him.

'Do you want me to be totally frank?'

The car dealer hesitated, and then nodded.

'You need an operation without delay,' the doctor said.

'And then?'

'And then we'll see.'

'Aha,' Burda realized, 'it's life or death, then?'

'None of us is here for ever,' the doctor said, 'but we must never give up hope. When they open you up, we'll know more.'

The car dealer knew, of course, that when his number came up that would be it, but he was shocked none the less. After all, he still had almost ten years to go before he attained the average life span for Czech men. He had always believed that death came most frequently in the form of a road accident. And he was an excellent driver.

'There are increasingly effective drugs around,' the doctor added, 'so don't give up hope.'

'As far as drugs are concerned, I can afford anything, however much it costs.'

'I know that,' said the doctor, 'but it's not a question of money.'

'What is it a question of, then?'

The doctor shrugged. 'Your resistance. The will of God, fate, or whatever you want to call it.'

The operation was arranged for the following week. In the meantime he would have to undergo all the necessary tests.

When Burda came home and his wife asked what the doctor had discovered, he answered laconically, 'I'm going to die.' Then he went to his room, sat down in an armchair and pondered on the strange fact that soon he might not be here any more. Human beings had always struck him as being like machines: machines and human beings wore out with use, but a machine could be kept going more or less indefinitely by replacing its parts. But how was it with a human being? It seemed so cruel and unjust that a dead machine could be virtually eternal, whereas human components were mostly non-renewable and people were therefore condemned to die before their time. Then he started to worry over what he would do about his property and with his secret bank accounts. When he died everything he owned would go to his wife and children. This seemed to him unjust because none of them had contributed towards the family income. And besides he had given his daughter a car not long ago – and his sons didn't want to know him. It was true that his wife took care of him, but he regularly gave her money for that and paid for her to go skiing in the Alps every winter and every spring. She was bound to have lovers all over the place, in fact he knew about one for sure. He had happened to come upon a letter from the man in his wife's handbag when he was looking for a bill or something. So why, in addition to all the property and money of his that she would inherit, should his wife get money that she didn't even know existed, just because he had married her?

Then he pondered on the doctor's words about hope and the will of God. To rely on the will of God was as pointless as trusting in fate. The will of God was just something to pacify the weak and the poor, whereas fate did what it was bribed to do. So far he had successfully bribed it and now he shied from the thought of drawing a total blank.

╱ That same afternoon, he climbed into his Mercedes, taking with him his passport and a suitcase, and set off for the border. There was only a hundred thousand francs in his Swiss account, but more in his German one. To the dismay of the teller he asked for it in cash. He returned with the money the next evening and hid the bank notes in a little safe to which he alone had the combination. The following day he went for his first test.

When he was about to go into hospital he was faced with the problem of what to do with the money. The doctor had warned him that he might be in for several weeks. That he might never leave was not mentioned, but the car dealer was all too aware that this possibility could not be ruled out. In fact he might never leave the operating theatre alive. He didn't feel like leaving the money at home, but he could hardly take it to the hospital. Where could he hide it? What would he do with it while he was lying unconscious on the operating table?

Eventually he made up his mind and divided up the hundred-thousand wads into smaller bundles which he stuffed into some old felt slippers and hid them with a pair of rolled socks. Then in his wife's presence he packed the slippers into a box and sealed it with sticking tape, asking her to bring it to the hospital along with a few other odds and ends, such as ordinary slippers, his toilet bag, two issues of a motoring magazine and his wallet with a few hundred crowns as soon as he asked for them.

He put aside a few thousand marks, sealing them in an envelope for the surgeon. However, the latter made some vague excuse about being superstitious and not wanting to hear about money before the operation, and refused to take the envelope from him.

When they opened Burda up on the operating table they discovered that the cancer had not only taken possession of his pancreas, it had also invaded other organs. A radical operation looked so hopeless that they simply sewed him back up again. After two days on the intensive care ward, he was transferred to ward eight which he shared with two other patients. The man to his left was an old blabbermouth from the country who spent most of his time telling trivial stories about his life back home and worrying over the fate of the smallholding that he had left his wife to look after on her own. In the bed to his right was an old man who said nothing and was most likely dying. Now and then, whether awake or asleep, he would produce strange, unintelligible animal-like screeches. These would disturb the car dealer even more than the smallholder's stories, which he simply ignored.

The doctors prescribed a great many drugs and once a day a nurse would bring a stand over to his bedside and hang a bottle from it. She would then insert a needle into one of his veins and he could watch the blood or some colourless liquid flow down the transparent tube and into his body. In spite of it, he felt more and more wretched with each passing day.

His wife brought him all the things he had asked for, adding a bunch of Gerbera and a jar of stewed fruit.

Flowers didn't interest him and he had lost all appetite for food. When his wife left, he opened the box with the slippers, took out the socks and checked that the wads of bank notes were there. He stuffed the socks back in, closed the box and hid it in his bedside table. He was still able to walk, but only to shuffle over to the window or into the corridor before returning to his metal bed. These days he didn't even like leaving the ward. His own death wasn't something he thought about as such, but he couldn't help noticing that his strength was steadily waning. Eventually he would have no strength left at all and he would close his eyes and be incapable of thinking or speaking, let alone taking decisions. What was he going to do with that money?

His wife visited him twice a week and sometimes his married daughter would look in as well. Once his elder son came. They would each bring something he had no use for and he would put it away in his bedside table without interest, and it would either stay there or he would take it and throw it in the waste bin as soon as they had gone.

There were several nurses on the ward. Apart from one older woman, they were hardly more than schoolgirls. They all seemed alike to him and he could only tell them apart by the colour of their hair. They treated him with professional kindness and sometimes would try to joke with him or cheer him up. Before sticking the needle into his vein they would apologize that it was going to hurt a little bit. But then a new nurse appeared – probably just back from leave. She seemed no older than the others, but he was immediately struck by her voice, which reminded him of the long-lost and almost forgotten voice of his mother. The nurse's name was Věra. He noticed that whenever she came over to him to do some routine job she would always find something to say. And to his surprise, it wasn't just the usual words of comfort, but something about the world outside; about the nice warm day, the jasmine in bloom or the strawberries already ripening on her balcony. He would listen to her, often unaware of what she was actually saying, conscious merely of the colour of her voice and its soothing quality.

One day when he was feeling slightly better after a blood transfusion, he tentatively asked her if she would come and sit by him.

'But Mr Burda,' she said in astonishment, 'what would Matron say if she caught me slacking?' None the less she brought a chair and sat down beside him, taking his hand, punctured with so many injections, and stroking the back of it.

'What sort of a life do you have, nurse?' he asked.

'What sort of a life?' she laughed. 'Average, I suppose.'

'Do you live with your parents?'

She nodded. She told him she had a little room in a block of flats. That the room contained just a bed, a chair, a bookshelf, and a bamboo stand with pots of flowers: a passion-flower, a fuchsia and a Crown of Thorns. She talked to him for a long time about flowers. Flowers had never interested him and their names evoked neither colours nor shapes, but he was conscious of the tenderness in the woman's voice and the gentle touch of her fingers on the back of his hand. He noticed that her eyes were dark brown even though she had naturally fair hair. She promised to bring him some of the flowers she grew on her balcony and then stood up and left.

The next day she really did bring him a lily and once again she came and sat by him.

He asked her if there was anything important that she lacked.

She didn't understand the meaning of his question.

So he asked her if she had a car.

'A car?' She laughed at the question.

'And would you like one?'

'You used to sell them, didn't you?' she recalled. Then she said she had never thought of having one. She lived with her mother and they scarcely had enough money to buy the occasional bag of tomatoes. Last year she had planted a few tomato plants on the balcony but they had been attacked by mould and there had been nothing to harvest. She asked him if he liked tomatoes. She asked him the way he used to ask people if they liked caviar or whether they preferred oysters. He replied that he liked them, although in fact he couldn't recall whether he had ever enjoyed them.

He was about to ask her if she found her life depressing, but at that moment he had a sudden spasm of pain and the nurse ran off to find a doctor who gave him an injection that left him groggy.

When he began to come round that night, he realized for the first time, with absolute urgency, that he was likely to die in the next few days. He switched on the light above his bed, leaned over and took the box of slippers out of his bedside table. Underneath the rolled socks lay a fortune that could buy whole wagonloads of tomatoes.

He tidied it all away again and returned the box to the bedside table; the wealth that usually imbued him with a sense of satisfaction was suddenly becoming a burden.

Should he give it to some charity? Or to the hospital? Give it to the doctors who weren't even capable of helping him? Or to his wife, so she could afford even more demanding lovers and go off skiing somewhere in the Rocky Mountains?

Then suddenly he could see the face of the nurse and hear the sound of her voice that so resembled his mother's. He wondered whether she would be on duty the next day and realized that he hoped she would.

She did come the next day and she brought him a tomato. It was large and firm and the colour of fresh blood. He thanked her. He bit into it and chewed the mouthful for a long time, but was unable to swallow it for fear of vomiting.

The nurse brought a stand over to his bed, attached a bottle and announced: 'We're going to have to feed you up a bit, Mr Burda. You're getting too weak.'

He nodded.

'Does your family visit you?' the nurse asked.

He ought to reply that he had no family, just a wife and three children, but instead he answered that it was a long time since anyone had visited him.

'They'll come soon,' the nurse said. 'That'll cheer you up.'

He closed his eyes.

She touched his forehead with her fingers. 'It's flowing now,' she said. 'God can work miracles and cure the sick as well as forgive the sinner. And He welcomes everyone with love.'

'Why?' he asked, and meant why was she telling him this, but she replied, 'Because God is love itself.'

In spite of the strong tablets they were giving him, he could not get off to sleep that night. He was thinking about the strange fact that the world would continue, that the sun would still go on rising, that cars would go on running, that they would go on dreaming up new types of car, that they would continue selling them in the showrooms that his wife would no doubt get rid of, that new motorways and overpasses would be built, that the Petřín tunnel would be opened, but he would never hear about any of them. That realization was like an icy hand gripping him by the throat. He tried to fight it, to find someone to help him but he had no one to turn to. Then the face of the nurse who had sat by his bed appeared to him, saying that God can welcome anyone with love. God could do it, though he himself had never been able to. That was if God existed. If He did, then at least a little bit of love would reign on earth. He tried to remember those he had ever loved or who had ever loved him. But apart from his mother, who had been dead for thirty years, he couldn't think of anyone. Tomorrow he would ask the nurse where she had come by her belief in God, or in love, at least. Finally he fell asleep. When he woke up in the middle of the night, an absurd idea struck him: he would give the money to the nurse. For telling him those things about God and love. For stroking his forehead even though she knew he was going to die. She was aware of it just as all the others were, but they didn't stroke his forehead.

Then he tried to imagine how she would respond to unexpected wealth. Would she accept it? In his experience, people never refused money. Outwardly they hesitated, but eventually they succumbed. He couldn't just stuff several million into her pocket, though; he would have to ask her to call a notary. He would dictate his will and leave the money to her. What would she do with it?

The following day, instead of questioning her about her beliefs, he asked her whether she lived only with her mother, or if she was going out with someone.

She stared in surprise, but she answered him. Her boyfriend's name was Martin and he was a violinist. They had been at a concert together the previous evening. It had been a performance of Beethoven's D Minor concerto. Did he know it? Did he like it?

He wasn't familiar with Beethoven, even though he must have heard the name some time. He had never had any time for music. There was always music playing in the showrooms, but it was pop music.

She went on to tell him that she and Martin were getting married in the autumn. 'Will you come to our wedding?' she asked.

'If you invite me.'

The next day nurse Věra was off duty, so he had a chance to reflect on whether he had thought things through clearly, and whether his decision hadn't been over-hasty. What if he got better? What if God were to perform a miracle or one of the medicines they were injecting into him restored his strength? Why else would the nurse have invited him to her wedding? She would hardly have been joking with a dying man.

Besides, the sum was disproportionately large, and there was the risk that his gift might make them suspect her of malpractice. But he could make her a gift of some of the money – at least that bundle of 1000-franc notes.

The next day his condition deteriorated but he was fully conscious of nurse Věra coming to him and putting some fresh flowers into a bottle of water, and then bringing over the stand and inserting a needle into his left leg.

'I'll make it up to you,' he said in an undertone.

'The way to make it up to me is by getting better,' she said. Then she opened the window and said, 'Can you smell it? The lime trees are in blossom already.'

He could smell nothing. He just felt an enormous weariness.

He ought to tell her to call the notary, but at that moment it occurred to him that the whole idea was ridiculous: he should simply put a few bank notes into the pocket of her overall. Even that would be a fortune as far as she was concerned.

The nurse stroked his forehead and went out of the room.

The next night Alois Burda died. Nurse Věra happened to be on duty and a few seconds before he took his last breath she came and sat near him and held his hand. By then it was unlikely that he even noticed.

Afterwards the nurse was given the job of removing the possessions from the dead man's bedside table and making a precise list of everything. She did so. The list had eighteen items; number eleven read: *One pair of felt slippers with one pair of socks inside*. The nurse was surprised at how heavy the slippers were and it occurred to her to take out the socks, list them separately and look inside the slippers, but she didn't as it would mean her adding another item to the list, and besides it seemed pointless to waste time on things that no one was likely to use any more.

When Burda's wife came to the hospital for the death certificate, they handed her a bag of the deceased's property and a list of its contents. His wife ran her eye down the list of things. In the last few years she had grown sick of her husband and the few pathetic items he had left behind sickened her even more. They handed her his wallet and the three hundred crowns. She took the bag and put it in the boot of her car. When she was driving away from the hospital she noticed an illegal rubbish tip. She pulled up in front of it and took a careful look around her. Then she opened the boot and tossed the bag onto the tip.

That evening nurse Věra had a date with her violinist. 'That Burda on ward eight went to the mortuary the night before last,' she announced. 'He was supposed to be horribly rich – one of the richest men in Prague.'

'And did he give you anything?'

'No,' she said, 'he only had three hundred crowns in his wallet.'

'Rich men tend to be strange,' he said. 'Who do you think he'll leave it all to?'

'Goodness knows,' she said. 'I don't think he had anyone. He had no one to come and hold his hand, not even for those last few moments.'

(1994)

THE WHITE HOUSE

A blind girl stood before the castle entrance playing the Amerindian melody 'El Condor Pasa' on the flute. A short distance away a coach full of foreigners pulled up and their guide started bellowing instructions into a megaphone. Japanese tourists swarmed from the bus and started taking photographs; someone started to play a hit song loudly on a radio. The sound of the flute was almost drowned out in the din, but the blind girl went on playing single-mindedly.

Jakub stopped a short way off. He liked the tune and he was also taken by the blind girl's tenacity. Maybe it wasn't tenacity but desperation. He found the girl attractive. Her hair was a blaze of coppery red, while her complexion seemed almost unhealthily pale. Her eyes were shut and her white stick was propped against the wall of the house. A small case lay in front of her with a few coins in it.

Jakub had had a successful day. Admittedly he was only a student of mathematics (though he also attended a few philosophy lectures), but he had just received an honour for his last exam and what's more he had just got a good deal for his step-father and been paid a decent commission for his pains. He pondered whether he should just give the girl a coin or even a bank note, but in the end he went over to her and said, 'You play really well. Could I invite you to dinner for that song?'

The girl turned her face to him. 'Is it me you are asking?' she said and blushed. She was wearing a cheap frock of flowery calico.

'There is no one else playing here.'

'There's always someone playing here every day from morning to night. And I don't even know you.'

So Jakub introduced himself.

'Why are you inviting me?'

'I told you. Because I like the way you play.'

'I'm not sure. I'm not sure,' she repeated. 'I don't want you to pity me. But you have a kind voice. May I touch your hand?'

Jakub gave her his hand but she didn't shake it. She ran the tips of her fingers over it as if by doing so she could tell if he wanted to harm her. She had long, fine fingers and her touch seemed tender to him. 'Okay', she said, 'but not to dinner, I couldn't accept that from you. What if we just go and sit somewhere and have a mineral water? Or a glass of wine, maybe?'

He took her to a Chinese restaurant, because he liked Chinese food and he had had a successful day. He also wanted to please her. Why her of all people? He had no girlfriend at the time, or anyone else he needed to please. He ordered duck done in some Chinese style (the girl declared she had never eaten anything like it, and he felt as flattered as if he had cooked the food himself) and some rice wine. So they became acquainted.

The girl's name was Alžběta and she was a year older than

Jakub. She had been blind from birth and there was no hope of her ever gaining her sight. From time to time she earned a bit of extra money by playing the flute, as the invalidity pension she received barely covered her rent and basic necessities. And sometimes she wanted to buy a cassette or CD or go to a concert. She also wanted to buy a new guitar.

Her eyes were a misty grey and Jakub had the impression that now and then she gazed at him fixedly, but then her eyes would assume an empty look. She was shy and often apologized, asking him repeatedly whether she wasn't keeping him or if he was bored.

Then he walked with her to the house where she lived. It was an ugly and shabby apartment house in a dirty street in Vršovice. When they were saying goodbye, she thanked him several times and then said, 'I shouldn't think we'll see each other again.'

What most surprised or even moved him about this little speech was the word 'see'. 'Why not?' he asked. 'I know where you live now.' And he gave her his address too.

A few days later he rang her doorbell and invited her out for a walk.

'Why did you come for me?' she asked.

He wasn't sure himself. But he replied, 'Because I wanted to see you.'

'I didn't expect you to come.' Then she let him take her by the hand and lead her. They walked as far as Gröbe Park. Spring was coming to an end: there was the scent of jasmine all along the path and the park was a riot of colour. They sat down on a bench and he tried to describe the city below them. But the city was a mixture of shapes and colours that she could not possibly comprehend. She recognized only sounds, scents and smells, and the only shapes she knew were the ones she could span with her fingers.

They talked about music and then Jakub tried to explain post-modernism to her. He told her he went horse-riding and mountaineering, and enjoyed playing basketball, as he was over six feet tall. Also, that he helped his step-father sell real-estate and that until the beginning of last spring he had been going out with his classmate Jitka.

Alžběta hadn't been going out with anyone – either last spring or the previous one. She played the flute, the violin and the guitar and had a good musical memory. She could memorize simple tunes at the first hearing; more difficult ones she needed to hear twice. She had a number of girlfriends, most of whom were blind as well. She also had two brothers who were older than herself and sighted.

He accompanied her as far as her house and then leaned over and kissed her on the hair. 'You have pretty hair.'

'So I've been told. Apparently it's the colour of flame.' She took his hand and pressed it. Then she stood on tiptoe and searched for his face with her hand. When she found his chin she stroked him from his mouth to the tips of his hair. 'Thank you,' she said.

'What are you thanking me for?'

'For today.'

'I didn't make it.'

'For me, you did.' She didn't ask if they'd see each other again and he didn't say anything either, but he came back two days later.

So the two of them started to go out together.

He wouldn't have been able to explain to anyone why he was going out with a blind girl, but then there is no explaining love, it simply happens. At first he was attracted by the fact that she moved in a different world, one without light or colour, a world full of hostile shapes and obstacles. In the days following their first encounter he tried to imagine that world. He stopped watching television and started to listen to the radio, partly so that he would be able to talk to her about various programmes. On his way home – he lived in a quiet residential area – he would try walking along the familiar footpath with his eyes closed. Sometimes he would even pick up a fallen branch and try to use it like a white stick. Even so he never managed to walk more than forty paces. Then he would stop and not dare take another step in the dark. A world without colour was like a black-and-white film, but even a black-and-white film made use of shapes. What shapes were there in her world? What were her dreams like? He would have liked to ask, but they got used to not talking about her blindness and she did her level best not to seem different in any way from other people. In fact, once when he took her with him to the riding school she asked if she could try riding a horse. He went along with her game that she differed in no way from him and explained to her what she must do in the saddle. Then he helped her mount one of the mildest tempered fillies and led her in a circle around the arena, while Běta, thanks to her natural sense of rhythm, jogged up and down in the saddle as if she was an avid watcher of Westerns.

'What colour is this filly?' she wanted to know.

'Brown.'

'I thought so.'

'Why?'

'Because she's warm.'

In an effort to become more familiar with his world, the

world of the sighted, she would ask about colours which she could only imagine as various degrees of warmth or cold. What was cold she perceived as white, what was hot as red, orange or yellow.

How would she perceive the yellowing leaves of the birch trees in autumn?

Most likely as the quietest of rustling in the breeze.

She also liked using words that belonged to the vocabulary of the sighted. 'I saw you in the distance,' she would say when they had a rendezvous somewhere. How could she see him in the distance? Only insofar as she could make out the sound of his footsteps.

She stopped in front of a flower-stall. 'Look at those beautiful fresh roses!'

How could she tell they were beautiful and fresh? By their scent maybe.

He was also moved by her gratitude for his love. 'Is it possible that you really love me?'

He assured her that it was.

'But why? You could have found so many sighted girls.'

He told her it didn't matter whether she could see or not.

'Why? With me you can do hardly any of the things you could with them.'

He told her that he particularly liked the fact that her world was different from his. On the contrary, uniformity was like death. In death everything and everyone became the same, didn't they?

'You'll leave me one day, anyway. But I don't want to think about it. You're with me now and I'm grateful to you for every second.'

'Don't thank me. I could just as easily thank you.'

'For what? For what?'

'For your love.'

'You can't thank me for that.'

'There you are, then.'

'I'm grateful to you anyway. Maybe I'll repay you one day. Either I will, or God will.'

'There's nothing to repay.' Then he said. 'Love can only be repaid with love.'

'I know. That's what I mean.'

Sometimes it struck him that her world, which lacked colours and clearly defined shapes, was no poorer than his own. It might be less colourful, but it was deeper and more intense. The same was true of her feelings and her capacity to experience things. He wasn't sure whether he would be capable of such depth, of concentrating on a piece of music, a thought, an experience or a feeling, the way she did. When he first met her he was ready to pity her. He liked the fact that he had to lean down to her, that he was giving her what nobody else would give her, but he could equally envy her and accept that she was giving him something that he would never find with a woman who was as frivolous as he was.

They listened to music together, walked together in the streets and parks, sipped wine in cheap little cafés (he was only a student, after all) and made love in his room, in the woods, or on a sun-warmed rock that she boldly clambered up with him.

Sometimes when they were parting, she would say softly, like a word of farewell, 'Don't leave me yet!' And he wasn't sure whether she meant that very moment or the next day; whether it was a quiet entreaty for him to come again. Usually he would kiss her then and tell her he wouldn't leave her.

He hadn't left her – so far, but as the summer went by

there was a waning of his enthusiasm for the impenetrable world of the blind. He was, after all, too attached to the hustle and bustle of the world of the sighted and more and more often he would be aware of what he was missing with a blind girl. He was also sure that he didn't want to live with her for the rest of his life, that it would be too much for him. He knew that one day, sooner rather than later, he would leave her. This realization did not unduly bother him: after all one lived for the present, not the future. People who worried too much about the future were incapable of experiencing the here and now. When the time came, most likely at the end of the holidays, they would simply stop seeing one another. It might be harder for Běta than for him, but it couldn't be helped.

Before the holidays were over he planned to go off to the Tatras with his mountaineering friends. He could simply tell Běta that he was going off for ten days, but subconsciously he felt that this would be a more final separation. After the holidays, his life would return to normal and she wouldn't fit into it somehow. He felt that he ought to think up a last treat for her, something special that they could both remember. He had had a warning dream in which he fell into a deep rocky chasm from which there was no escape. Even though he wasn't superstitious and the dream could easily be interpreted as suppressed anxiety, it was a good pretext for him to change his travel plans. He set off with Běta for the Silica plateau area of Southern Slovakia. They found a room in a little inn near the station. The countryside was almost flat but dotted here and there with limestone outcrops or seemingly bottomless ravines.

The morning after their arrival was sultry, a sign of an impending storm, but in spite of this they decided to go into the forest to escape the heat. The forest lay close to the village and extended way beyond the Hungarian border.

They climbed a stony footpath that was already scorching hot from the morning sun and entered the woods. As long as they kept to the path he didn't even need to lead her by the hand. She only needed to hear the sound of his footsteps ahead of her.

The path was narrow and in places it disappeared in the grass. They reached a cross-roads: one path sloped gently uphill and he chose that one. She followed him obediently like a blind puppy. What would become of her if he lost her? She'd die, most likely. What would happen if he were to injure himself in some way and they couldn't go on? They'd both die, probably. Strange hollows started to appear at each side of the path, as if someone had forced the land into a powerful press and it was beginning to burst.

He took Běta by the hand for safety. The forest became darker and there was the sound of distant thunder. At the next cross-roads he started to become anxious. They ought to make their way back but he was no longer sure of the right direction. He took one of the paths and guided her along it until eventually the track ended in a kind of wooded gorge.

Then it started to rain. He found shelter beneath a tall beech tree with dense foliage. The rain and the darkness became more intense and when they set off again an hour later they were stiff and soaked to the skin, and to make it worse he had no idea which direction they should take. He set off aimlessly along sodden paths that would peter out unexpectedly or become totally lost in the high untrodden grass.

Ashamed to admit he was lost he just plodded on this way and that. The rain hissed loudly in the treetops, but otherwise there was only the sound of their own footsteps. Neither of them spoke. At last she said, 'Don't get upset and don't worry about me. I don't mind the rain.'

'That's good.'

Nevertheless he felt a growing sense of irritation. If he were on his own he would be able to cope. He'd run or keep going in the same direction regardless of the conditions underfoot. Instead he had to lead this sightless girl by the hand and whenever they came to a dead end he had to go back and find another path. As time went on he realized that they had not seen anyone along the way and if they ended up going deeper into the forest along the frontier they might not find a way out before evening. How much longer would that frail creature manage to stumble along paths that were full of snares for her? He couldn't abandon her. He couldn't say to her: wait there, I'll come back for you, because he couldn't be certain of finding her again. What he was certain of was that she wouldn't be able to find the way on her own.

They came to a kind of hollow from which water now overflowed. Water always flowed in one direction so if he managed to follow it they must eventually come out somewhere.

For a while he led Běta through boulders and slithered with her down a steep hillside before discovering that the water, as often happens in limestone country, suddenly disappeared underground. He halted. 'Shall we rest here a moment?'

'We don't have to on my account.' Then she asked, 'Are you lost?'

'It looks like it.'

'Are we deep in the forest?'

'How should I know? I haven't the foggiest idea where we are.'

She pressed herself to him. 'Don't be cross with me. Up there,' she said, pointing up the overgrown gorge, 'I can see a house. A white house.'

He looked in the direction she was pointing. All he could see were the rainswept tops of broad-leaved trees and a white boulder gleaming in their midst.

'That's a rock,' he snapped. 'There's no house there.'

'Yes, there's a rock and the house is behind it. Perhaps we could shelter in it.'

'We can't shelter in a house that doesn't exist. How can you tell me you can see something?'

'I'm sorry. I know I can't really see anything. It just seemed to me there was a house.'

It made little difference now which way they went. Although there was no path leading in that direction, he took her by the hand and, almost with a sense of relish, dragged her uphill through the bushes. She tripped on tree roots and got caught up in the long thorny creepers. He disentangled her crossly.

'Are you very cross with me?'

'No, but it's pouring with rain and we're both soaked to the skin.'

'And I'm holding you back.'

'Don't talk about that . . .'

'When we get home . . .'

'If we get home!'

'We'll reach it in a moment.'

'What, the white house? You can shut up about that at least.'

'Don't be cross with me. When we get back to the inn, you can put me on the train and I'll go back to Prague. I won't be in your way any more.'

He ought to say he wouldn't do anything of the sort, but he remained silent. He imagined what a relief it would be to put her on a train and be free of the burden.

They clambered on until at last they reached the ridge. The woods on the opposite slope were sparse and not far below them he could make out the low wall of a cemetery. Beyond it, away from the gravestones, the low, newly painted mortuary shone white. He stood, gaping at it in amazement.

'Is something the matter?' she asked.

'You must see it now, even I can.'

'Is it white?'

'White and cold.'

'Do you think we'll find shelter there?'

'I expect it's locked.'

'Doesn't anyone live there?'

'No, this isn't a place for the living.'

'Is it a cemetery?'

'Yes.'

'Then there must be a path leading to it.'

'All paths lead to it.'

'I didn't mean it that way. Are you angry?'

'Me, with you?'

'Everything's more difficult with me tagging along, you know that. You could have been home ages ago.'

They reached the cemetery wall. A pavement led to it from the other side. 'I wouldn't want to be home now.'

'Thank you,' she said.

'What for? You found the path.'

'You didn't leave me.'

He stopped and looked at her. Her weary face was soaking wet and a trickle of blood ran from a fresh scratch beneath her unseeing left eye. Her hair had darkened and lost its fiery colour.

'Are you looking at me?'

'How can you tell? Can you see everything?'

'I can't see anything. I just sense things.'

'Did you sense the cemetery too?'

'I sensed that I loved you.'

'I want to say something to you. Something important.'

She seemed to him to cower, as if to ward off a blow, as if she knew what had been going through his mind not so long ago.

'Don't leave me!' he said.

(1994)